Saving Mistletoe

A Sweet Holiday Novella

by
SHANNA HATFIELD

Saving Mistletoe

ISBN-13: 978-1979857154
ISBN-10: 1979857156

Shanna Hatfield
shanna@shannahatfield.com
shannahatfield.com

Cover Design by Shanna Hatfield

*To those who are willing
to make a change
that can change the world
around them...*

Books by Shanna Hatfield

FICTION

CONTEMPORARY

Blown Into Romance
Love at the 20-Yard Line
Learnin' the Ropes
QR Code Killer
Rose
Saving Mistletoe
Taste of Tara

Rodeo Romance
The Christmas Cowboy
Wrestlin' Christmas
Capturing Christmas
Barreling Through Christmas
Chasing Christmas

Grass Valley Cowboys
The Cowboy's Christmas Plan
The Cowboy's Spring Romance
The Cowboy's Summer Love
The Cowboy's Autumn Fall
The Cowboy's New Heart
The Cowboy's Last Goodbye

Silverton Sweethearts
The Coffee Girl
The Christmas Crusade
Untangling Christmas

Women of Tenacity
A Prelude
Heart of Clay
Country Boy vs. City Girl
Not His Type

HISTORICAL

Hardman Holidays
The Christmas Bargain
The Christmas Token
The Christmas Calamity
The Christmas Vow
The Christmas Quandary
The Christmas Confection

Pendleton Petticoats
Dacey
Aundy
Caterina
Ilsa
Marnie
Lacy
Bertie
Millie
Dally

Baker City Brides
Tad's Treasure
Crumpets and Cowpies
Thimbles and Thistles
Corsets and Cuffs
Bobbins and Boots

Hearts of the War
Garden of Her Heart
Home of Her Heart

Chapter One

Portland, Oregon

"No, no, no, no," Ellen Meade chanted, glaring at the blank, black screen of her cell phone in disgust. Hadn't she charged it just a few hours ago? With her luck, the charger hadn't been fully plugged in and she'd failed to notice in her haste to get out the door.

What else could go wrong? This day, this whole disastrous week, or was it year, might give her ulcers if she survived it.

She stopped on the downtown Portland sidewalk and glanced around. Although she was only a dozen or so blocks from her office, she hadn't visited this particular part of town for a long time and had no idea how to find her client.

With the client's address and phone number trapped in her dead phone, along with directions on how to find Mr. Smith's office, she experienced a moment of panic. Situations like this never happened to her. Ellen was always organized. Always. She planned everything with care and foresight, leaving no room for surprises or failures.

Yet, despite her best efforts, nothing had gone according to plan recently.

Last year, her best friend had gone to Atlanta for a brief visit, fallen in love with some hunky horse wrangler who turned out to be a wealthy plantation owner, and married him a short time later. Tara and Brett were the epitome of wedded bliss, especially with a baby on the way.

Not that Ellen begrudged her friend a single second of happiness. Truly, she was thrilled Tara was living out her happily ever after, even if it was in Georgia and Ellen remained in Oregon.

When they were younger, dreaming of how they would take life by storm, Ellen had set her goals and achieved them with startling precision. The list of achievements she pursued wasn't long or complicated: graduate from high school with honors, earn a full scholarship to college, graduate at the top of her class, pass the bar exam, take a job with a firm that guaranteed promotions and prestige, earn a partnership and get married — all before she turned twenty-six.

After celebrating her birthday two weeks ago, she'd felt the twinges of disappointment plucking at her soul. She'd failed to live up to her own expectations. Without a boyfriend in sight, the possibility of getting married seemed even more far-fetched than gaining a partnership at the firm where she worked.

The partnership that opened up last month went, of course, to the nephew of one of the founding partners. The man was severely lacking brain cells, but Ellen couldn't very well tell her boss that. She supposed they'd figure it out soon enough. In the meantime, she assumed additional responsibilities in her already overwhelming workload, including meeting with this client whom she had no idea how to find.

A quick glimpse at her watch confirmed she had less than ten minutes to find the building or she'd be late.

What she wouldn't give for the good old days when public telephones, and telephone books, could be found every few blocks. If she had access to one, she could call her client. As it was, she knew she should have written down the address instead of relying solely on her phone.

The July sun beat down on her in an unexpected heat wave. Sweat trickled between her shoulder blades and slithered along her spine, increasing her discomfort. She should have taken a cab, one with air conditioning. Instead, she'd decided to enjoy the beautiful weather and take in the blue skies, blooming flowers, and sweetness of summer on a stroll to meet Mr. Smith. Now she was overheated, anxiety-plagued, dripping sweat, and about to be unforgivably late.

"This is just perfect," she muttered, dropping her phone inside the leather bag she carried over her shoulder before adjusting the bag's strap.

"Think, think, think," she said, rubbing her temple with one hand and closing her eyes.

Her mind drew a blank. Not so much as a hint of the address came to her. No sudden recall pointed her in the right direction. No burst of brilliance helped her remember the client's phone number.

Frustrated and resolved to returning to her office to retrieve the information she needed, she spun around and smacked into something warm and extremely solid. Momentarily stunned, she was afraid of what she'd hit. She cringed as she considered the possibilities of what she'd done.

The scent of leather and a man's masculine fragrance mingled with an aroma she vaguely recalled from summer camp when she was thirteen. She'd spent six weeks learning how to ride a horse among the other activities.

What in the world was a horse doing in downtown Portland and how had she blindly smacked into it?

Slowly opening her eyes, she glanced up at the scowling, tanned face of a police officer as he sat astride his large chestnut mount. The horse shook his mane and glanced back at her, as though he measured her worth and found her severely lacking.

She pushed against the man's muscled thigh to regain her balance and took a step back. The contact with his leg left her further unsettled than she'd been mere seconds before.

Who had muscles like that, anyway? His thigh felt like it was made of steel. What was the guy, a fitness nut? The short sleeves of his uniform shirt only accented his biceps and broad shoulders.

A brief perusal that started at the top of his hat and ended at the toes of his shiny leather riding boots confirmed that the man was, indeed, in prime physical shape.

His gaze held a hint of scorn as he continued to stare at her with a disapproving frown.

"May I help you, miss?" he asked in a smooth voice that held the hint of a drawl. He didn't sound Southern, exactly, but he wasn't from Portland, that was for sure. The man had a rugged, outdoorsy look to him. His seat on the back of the tall horse only accentuated the persona.

"No, thank you," she said. Another step back nearly carried her into two businessmen walking past her. One of them gave her a cool glare while the other shot her an interested glance.

"Are you sure, miss? You seem to be a little lost." The officer's expression didn't soften as he held her gaze with eyes that were a surprisingly clear shade of blue. In spite of his gruffness, Ellen couldn't help but notice the sculpted firmness of his lips, particularly the top one.

Unbidden, thoughts of kissing it flew into her head. The only explanation she could latch onto was the possibility she had lost her mind. That had to be it. Stress, too many hours on the job, and the fact her last real date had been back in college definitely contributed to her current enthralled state.

The officer leaned down from the saddle, studying her. "Are you an attorney?" The frown lines on his forehead deepened and angry sparks ignited in his eyes.

Shocked by his question, Ellen mutely nodded.

"Did you defend Jonathan Westmont a few months ago?" he asked, a hard edge seeping into his tone.

"As a matter of fact, I did." Ellen couldn't think of any reason this officer would know who she was, unless... She took a moment to picture him in a dress uniform, with fury riding his features as he offered testimony at the trial. If his hostile glares could have brought about her demise, she wouldn't have made it out of the courtroom alive. The high-profile case and the fact she'd won earned her a hefty promotion and a promise she'd be considered the next time a partnership became available.

Ellen had experienced her share of doubts about her client's innocence. However, her job wasn't to judge him, but defend him. She'd done her job exceptionally well. Hopefully, her client would learn from his near miss with a prison cell as his abode and not find himself in a similar mess in the future.

"Johnnie Westmont is as guilty as sin and thanks to you the people he cheated won't ever get their money back, or have any closure on the devastation he caused." The officer straightened and gave her a loathsome look. "Not only that, but it's just a matter of time before he does it again. You should feel proud of yourself for making certain a criminal was allowed to go free. If he's the poster child for the types of people you represent, how do you sleep at night?"

"Why do you seem to have such a vested, personal interest in him, sir?" Ellen asked, affronted. In spite of her irritation, her curiosity sought satisfaction. What did it matter to Officer Handsome-And-Hotheaded? How dare he condemn her for doing her best for the client?

"I don't have a personal interest in him, but anyone smarter than an idiot could see he was guilty. One of his victims just happens to be a friend of mine. And I'm the one who found out about his scheme, which is why I testified." He gave her a long, observant glance. "Is there some reason you're wandering around here? Do you need assistance? Escorted somewhere? Arrested for assaulting an officer?"

From the dark look on his face, she got the idea helping her might give the man an acute case of indigestion. No doubt lingered in her mind that he'd take great pleasure in hauling her in and locking her in a jail cell.

"No thank you, Officer," she snapped and turned back in the direction she'd originally headed. Conscience pricked by his condemnation, she didn't want to think about all the concerns his questions stirred.

In fact, sleep had become an elusive wish at night since she'd accepted her first promotion at the firm. The higher up the ladder she climbed, the more she felt urged to leave behind the moral and ethical compasses that had always guided her. She didn't like representing clients she thought were guilty, but when her boss told her to take a case, she took it without question.

Lately, it was getting harder and harder to help clients she knew were scamming, cheating, lying scum dressed in expensive suits.

Ellen had such big dreams, such high hopes about being a high-powered, successful attorney. Now, her dreams inched toward delusions while the power she'd fought hard to gain seemed false and empty at best.

Regardless, it wasn't any of the police officer's business and today wasn't the day to allow her mind and heart to engage in a heated debate.

Even if she was lost, she refused to admit to him how badly she needed to find her client's office. Her boss had stressed the importance of keeping Mr. Smith happy. Ellen had a feeling showing up late wouldn't sit well with the man.

The clip clop of the horse's hooves on the sidewalk kept step behind her as she marched forward, with no idea where she needed to go. Half a block later, she tossed a glance over her shoulder to find the officer and horse right behind her. She took a step to the right and stopped, turning back with an accusatory glower.

"Is there some reason you are following me?" she asked, indignant and growing annoyed.

"Who says I'm following you. I'm on duty and this is part of the area I'm patrolling today." He smirked. "Are you sure you don't need help?"

Ellen swallowed her pride and narrowed her gaze. "Do you know where to find the office of Smith and Matlock? They have an investment firm somewhere in this area."

The officer nodded. "I sure do."

Out of patience, Ellen wanted to stamp her foot. "And? Where can I find it?"

Those enticing lips curved upward in an almost grin as he pointed to a building across the street. "Right there."

"Oh." Ellen looked at the building, noticing the sign out front and the street numbers that jangled in her memory. "Thank you, Officer…"

"Tipton, miss. Burke Tipton." With surprising politeness, he tipped his hat to her then rode away.

Ellen watched him until he turned a corner before racing across the street. As she hurried onto the elevator, she pondered if she'd see the cranky officer again and felt vexed that she wanted to.

Chapter Two

Burke Tipton tightened the cinch on his saddle and dropped the stirrup then patted the neck of his red chestnut gelding.

"Ready to go, Sugar Bear?" he asked, wishing he'd never allowed his younger sister to name the horse. He'd tried to convince her that the name was better suited for a mare, but Bella wouldn't listen to him. Since he always kept his promises, his horse was stuck with the moniker. It hadn't been so bad before Burke joined Portland's Mounted Patrol Unit. But the other officers had nearly laughed him and Bear right out of the barn when they learned the horse's name.

Four years ago, Burke had requested a transfer to MPU from his regular beat with the Portland Police Bureau because he missed riding every day. He'd grown up on a ranch in Eastern Oregon where riding a horse was as second nature to him as brushing his teeth in the morning. It only took a few weeks before he worked up the nerve to ask the sergeant in charge if he'd consider allowing Burke to use his own horse. Sugar Bear passed the entry test with high scores. From that day on, they'd been an inseparable team.

Burke loved working with the horse he'd trained from the day Bear was born.

Burke swung into the saddle with ease then adjusted his seat. He'd gotten used to the Australian stock saddles MPU used on patrol, but he preferred to use his western saddles.

Although he'd been gone from the ranch for eight years, he still yearned for the wide-open spaces, clean air, and peacefulness he found there.

Nevertheless, he loved his job, loved doing something he felt was of value and of service. Growing up, he'd never once considered becoming a police officer. A month into his junior year of college, he couldn't shake the feeling he was meant to be doing something different than the career path he'd chosen. Eager to be a game warden, he ignored the prompting to become a police officer.

Finally, he gave in to the relentless inner calling and enrolled at the Police Academy. Of course, it meant dropping out of college, enraging his parents, and saying goodbye to his girlfriend who had deemed him "beyond nuts." In spite of those who failed to support him, Burke graduated at the top of his class. Once he started working patrols, he finished the criminal justice degree he'd originally been working toward through online classes.

Now, with autumn colors filling the landscape around him, there was no place he'd rather be than on patrol with Bear. October had arrived with beautiful, warm weather, the kind that made him glad he could spend the next ten hours working outside.

If the day had been cold and rainy, he might not have been quite as anxious to get to work. Even then, he just pulled on his rain gear and went about his day.

"What do you think, Bear?" Burke asked, and patted the horse on the neck again. "See anything amiss?"

The horse shook his mane and continued walking down the broad sidewalk toward the heart of downtown where Burke would spend the day on patrol.

In the distance, he could see two men arguing and gave Bear a little pressure from his knees, urging him forward. Before he could reach them, a woman darted around the corner of a building and slammed into his leg. The force knocked her backward and she fell to the sidewalk. The files she carried flapped open and papers scattered in the breeze like jumbo-sized snowflakes.

Burke jumped out of the saddle and knelt beside her as she looked at him with a dazed expression. He held back a groan as recognition set in. The last thing he needed was to have the snippy, beautiful attorney who willingly defended crooks bump into him, again.

What was it with her blindly walking into him and Bear? Maybe the woman needed glasses, although he'd hate to see anything cover up those mesmerizing whiskey-colored eyes.

Small of stature, it wasn't any wonder she'd landed on her backside as hard as she hit his leg. The tidy knot of hair pinned up on her head listed to one side, giving her a comical appearance. He tamped down his urge to laugh and gave her a questioning glance.

"Are you hurt, miss?" he asked, keeping his voice low and soothing.

"I... I don't think so." All at once, she snapped out of her trance and noticed the papers from her files floating all around them. "Oh, my files!" she gasped, struggling to rise.

Burke took her hand in his and stood, pulling her upright. Together, they quickly gathered the papers and she stuffed them back into a folder.

He offered her a stern glare as he handed her the last few wayward sheets. "I ought to write you a ticket, Miss Meade. If you don't start paying attention to where you're going, you could really hurt yourself or someone else."

Surprised at his gruff tone and sharp words, she lifted a curious gaze to his. "What, exactly, would you write on the ticket, Officer Tipton?"

The fact she recalled his name pleased him more than it should have. He mustered a fierce scowl, but then he looked into her face. Dang, she sure had gorgeous eyes. And her skin appeared silky smooth. Then there were those soft pink lips just begging for a kiss.

Man, he needed to get his head on straight, at least where this woman was concerned. "You're a public menace. This is the second time you've run into me. I could haul you in for assaulting not one but two officers if I wanted to," he warned. "Do you make it a habit of plowing into people, objects, and animals?"

Deep crimson blossoms gave away her embarrassment as she tugged the files closer against her chest, as though she could use them as a barrier to protect herself from his accusations.

"I... I'm not... I didn't." She closed her eyes and took a deep breath before she opened them again. "I'm sorry, Office Tipton. I was late for a meeting with a client and was reviewing the case as I walked. As for me making a habit of running into others, I can honestly say, you and your horse are the only two who've had to endure my bumbling moments. Please accept my apologies."

Taken aback by her apology and the sincerity in her voice, Burke didn't know what to say. He'd expected her to lambast him as she had the last time they'd met, or toss him an insufferable scowl.

Instead, she picked up the leather bag she'd dropped on the sidewalk, offered him a brief nod, and started to walk off.

"Miss Meade?" he called, not certain what urged him to call out to her. He could easily have let her go, but he didn't.

She stopped and turned back to face him. "Yes, sir?"

Humility covered her like a cloak while kindness seeped from warm, gleaming eyes that would no doubt invade his dreams. She seemed so different from the woman he'd seen in July. That girl had been cocky and full of herself, of the importance of her position and the power that accompanied it.

How could a few months make such a difference? The expensive suit she wore was similar to the one she had on the last time he'd seen her. The bag was the same one she'd toted then. He couldn't put his finger on what, exactly, was different about her. Only that something had undeniably altered in her world.

Unsettled by the changes he sensed in her, he waggled a finger in the direction of her head. "If you're meeting with a client, you might want to fix your hair."

"My hair?" she asked, then reached up and felt the knot that had slid far to the side. A sigh accompanied the roll of her eyes as she pulled out the pins and dropped them into an exterior pocket of her bag.

She ran her hand into the dark tresses and shook them loose. Her hair cascaded around her shoulders and down her back in a gleaming mass that made Burke's hands itch to touch it.

"Thanks for telling me. I'd hate to go to an appointment looking like a complete mess." She offered him a smile.

"Are you certain you aren't hurt, Miss Meade?" he asked, taking a step closer to her.

"I'm certain, Officer. Other than a dent to my pride and a bruise to my backside, I'm fine." Her cheeks flamed with color again at the admission and she hastily turned around. "I'm sorry about running into you and your horse. He's a beauty."

"He's not the only one," Burke muttered as she offered him a wave and rushed down the sidewalk. He swung onto Bear, wishing he could have offered to inspect her bruises.

A firm mental shake failed to dislodge thoughts of the woman. The remainder of the day, he pondered what might have happened to change the young attorney. For her sake, he hoped it wasn't something horrible and earth-shattering, like loss of a loved one or the diagnosis of a terminal illness.

The more he thought about the possibilities, the more concerned he grew. No reasonable explanation existed why he couldn't stop thinking of her. He'd been livid after she'd helped that jerk Jonathan Westmont avoid going to jail for bilking good people out of their hard-earned dollars. In truth, it wasn't her specifically he was angry with, but a system that sometimes failed to deliver justice.

He believed in the system, would give his life defending it if he needed to, but it bothered him when people like Westmont got away with crimes that created such hardships for others. Burke wouldn't have known anything about the man, except he had an elderly neighbor who'd invested his money in something that sounded fishy.

One day, he just happened to find himself in the same restroom downtown as Westmont and overheard the man bragging to a colleague about the millions he'd taken from "people too dumb to know better."

Burke was so angry when he realized the braggart was Westmont, he wanted to shove the man's head through a wall. Instead, he reported what he heard to his superiors. Detectives had already gathered enough evidence to make an arrest. Burke's testimony should have been the final nail in Westmont's coffin.

Yet, despite the proof that showed Westmont as guilty, he'd gotten off with nothing more than a few fines and a warning from the judge.

At the time, Burke had blamed Westmont's attorney. She'd looked so lovely, sweet, and innocent, he was convinced she'd swayed the jury into believing the crook was innocent. He'd thought her girl-next-door act was just that — an act.

Then she'd run into him, literally, in July. She'd looked the same then as she had at the trial. A little more harried, hurried, and worried, perhaps, but the same innocent girl.

That day, she'd turned around and bumped against his leg. It hadn't hurt him or Bear, but when she'd placed her hand on his thigh to get her balance, it felt like she pressed a hot brand to his skin. He'd even looked down to make sure she didn't have some sort of weapon in her hand.

Disturbed by the surge of emotions she evoked in him, he'd relied on his anger to mask everything else. Looking back, he'd probably been a little rude to her that day, but he was still mad over the whole debacle with Westmont. Burke's neighbor lost his entire life savings and had to take a job at a discount store just to keep a roof over his head. The man should have been more careful about investing his money, that was true, but it still didn't excuse Westmont from taking advantage. It certainly didn't excuse Miss Meade from helping Westmont go free when he ought to be rotting in jail.

If Burke cared to confess it, which he did not, he'd thought of the pretty attorney numerous times since their encounter on that hot summer day.

To see her again only stirred his interest in her. Perhaps his memory was faulty, but she looked even lovelier than he recalled. And she smelled nice, too. Like something that put him in mind of Christmas, although he couldn't say what it was.

It was ridiculous to think about hot chocolate, cozy fires, and peppermint-laced kisses when it was nearly eighty degrees outside and the trees bore the fiery splendor of autumn.

"Bear, I think I need a vacation," he grumbled to the horse as they made their way to the end of the patrol for the day.

The horse blew out a puff of air and shook his head, as though he disagreed.

"What do I need then, boy? Huh?"

The horse bobbed his head, as though trying to point Burke in the right direction.

There, at a vendor cart on the corner in front of him, was none other than Miss Meade. She searched through a selection of autumn-hued bouquets of flowers.

"Oh, come on," Burke groaned, tilting his gaze skyward. What were the odds of running into the woman twice in one day? Perched on the back of a big red horse, it wasn't like he could just casually walk by her unnoticed.

Resigned to speaking to her, he and Bear made their way down the sidewalk. Miss Meade gave him a passing glance. Eyes wide with surprise, she turned his way again and she studied him a moment. "Are you following me, Officer Tipton?"

"No, Miss Meade, I am not," he said, unable to hold back a grin. "Did you make it to your appointment on time?"

"Barely. I only had five minutes to spare." She handed cash to the vendor and accepted a large bouquet of burgundy and yellow autumn flowers.

"I take it you like to be punctual?" he asked, allowing Bear to move forward when Miss Meade thanked the vendor and began walking down the sidewalk.

"Ten minutes early, but I guess you can call that punctual since most people show up at least fifteen minutes late these days. I don't understand that at all." She stopped and observed the horse for a moment. "May I pet him?"

"Sure. He enjoys the attention," Burke said, keeping a firm hand on the reins as the attorney reached out a steady hand and let Bear take in her scent before she gently rubbed his face.

The horse blew out a contented sigh and fluttered his eyelashes.

She smiled and looked up at Burke. "He's a sweetheart. What's his name?"

"Sugar Bear."

At her barely constrained laugh, Burke grinned again. "Go ahead and laugh. I call him Bear, to salvage his pride and mine. I should never have promised my little sister she could name him."

"Your sister? Is she an officer, too?"

He shook his head. "No. Miss Bella just started her senior year of college at Oregon State University. She's planning to be a math teacher."

"A girl who loves math?" Miss Meade asked. "That's awesome. Math was never my strongest subject."

"Mine either," Burke admitted.

"But I still don't understand how your sister named a patrol horse?" She gave him a confused look.

"Sugar Bear is my horse. I grew up on a ranch in Eastern Oregon and raised him from the day he entered the world. He just happens to also be my work partner."

She smiled. "How wonderful for you both."

Her attention remained focused on Bear, so Burke cleared his throat, scrambling to keep the conversation going. "Are you finished with work for the day?"

"Yes. I'm on my way home." She pointed to an apartment building visible down the street. "It's not far."

"Mind if I accompany you? Bear and I are heading off our shift, too."

"It's a free world," she said, giving Bear another gentle rub before she stepped back and shifted the flowers, two reusable tote bags, and her leather bag.

Burke swung off the horse and held out a hand. "May I help you carry something?"

"Oh, that's okay, Officer Tipton. I'll manage." Her smile melted some of his reserve and most of his inclination to hold a grudge against the woman for past transgressions.

"I'm sure you can manage, but since I'm heading that way, I might as well lend a hand." He took the two tote bags from her, surprised by the weight in the bags. "What have you got in here? Rocks? Bricks?"

"Books, bagels, and dinner." She laughed. "Quite a combination, isn't it?"

As the autumn sunlight sent shards of golden light through her rich brown locks, the fascinating gleam and his desire to touch a wavy strand left him uncomfortable and concerned. With Bear's reins in one hand and the woman's bags in the other, he kept step with her the few blocks to her apartment building.

Glad to see it had a security fence around it, he let her take the bags from him after she punched in her code and the gate opened. "Thanks for the escort, Officer."

"My pleasure, Miss Meade." He took a step back and tipped his hat to her. "Have a pleasant evening, Miss Meade."

"Oh, for heaven's sake, call me Ellen. After I've smashed into you and sweet Sugar Bear twice, I think you can certainly call me by my first name."

"Okay, Ellen," Burke said, testing out her name and finding he liked the way it sounded on his tongue and echoed in his heart. Her name seemed a little old-fashioned, rather like the girl who possessed it. "Be careful. No more running into horses or police officers."

"I wouldn't dream of it, Officer Tipton." Her smile turned her from pretty to breathtakingly beautiful, accenting the fine lines of her cheekbones and the whiteness of her smile.

"If I'm supposed to call you Ellen, you might as well call me Burke, at least when I'm not on duty."

"But you're still on duty, sir." She stepped inside the gate and it slowly closed.

An odd bereft feeling swept over him as she stood out of his reach. "I'll bc off duty as soon as I get this guy settled in for the night." He let his gaze rove over that glorious head of hair, her sweet face, and down her conservative navy blue suit before returning to her face. "Take care, Ellen."

"I will, Officer… Burke."

He watched her walk away and enter the building through a side door. It had been on the tip of his tongue to ask her out, but he'd somehow managed to hold himself back. Even if he sensed a change in her, it didn't mean he planned to consort with her type. He wanted nothing to do with anyone who helped criminals go free.

Ellen held her breath until she stepped inside the apartment building. She could feel the officer's gaze on her back as she walked across the parking lot.

Burke Tipton was handsome, rugged, masculine, and apparently not quite as fierce and intimidating as she recalled from their July encounter.

She'd thought him uncommonly rude then, even as his words pricked her conscience. In truth, Burke was the reason she'd recently made so many changes in her life. Unable to stop thinking about his accusations, she knew what he said was true. Whether wittingly or not, she had helped criminals go free by defending them, purely focused on winning the trial, regardless of who it might hurt or harm. Her sole interest was not in her clients or the victims, but in making her employers happy so she could continue climbing up the corporate ladder.

After one particularly stressful day when she was asked to take on a client whom Ellen could tell was lying about his innocence before a minute of conversation had passed, she knew she'd had enough.

Enough of the lies, of working so hard for something that held no meaning, of pretending she was doing something good and purposeful with her life.

Thanks to Officer Tipton and his angry reaction to her, she'd opened her eyes and started herself down a new path.

Now, she couldn't help but wish her path would intersect his again. She'd like the opportunity to tell him how profoundly his words had changed her life. A sly smile filled her face as she realized she wouldn't begrudge another chance to see the good-looking officer.

Chapter Three

Burke impatiently drummed his fingers on the red and white checkered tablecloth at the pizza parlor and looked at the big clock on the wall for the tenth time in as many minutes.

One of his friends had practically begged him to go out on a date with a cousin, but so far, the girl had been a no-show. Maybe she was as reluctant to participate in a blind date as Burke was.

The past few months, Liam had mentioned his cousin with increasing frequency, which struck Burke as odd. He'd never heard Liam talk about the woman before, but his friend made it sound like a matter of life and death that Burke go out with her, the sooner the better. When Burke failed to show an appropriate measure of interest or urgency, Liam had pleaded with him to have dinner with the girl Friday night.

Burke had first met Liam at the gym years ago. Sometimes they played basketball together with a community team. Once in a while, they stopped for a burger after work and watched a football game on TV. In all the time he'd known Liam, the man had never asked him for a favor, so Burke didn't feel he could refuse when Liam insisted on the blind date.

The cousin was supposed to meet him at six at a popular pizza parlor, but the hands on the clock edged toward a quarter past the hour. In the grand scheme of things, she wasn't that late, but Burke was eager to latch onto any excuse to cancel the date and leave. The last thing he wanted was to spend his evening entertaining some girl who was clearly desperate enough to agree to Liam's matchmaking efforts.

He had no idea what she looked like, or even her full name. Liam just referred to her as EJ. He promised Burke meeting the cousin would be a pleasant surprise. Liam assured him she'd be easy to pick out in the crowd with a bright red and green scarf around her neck.

Although he seriously doubted the surprise would be pleasant, Burke remained seated at his table. He flagged down a server and ordered another Dr. Pepper then leaned back in the chair, waiting for his date.

A minute later, he glanced up and saw Ellen Meade hurry inside the busy restaurant. Cheeks and nose red from the cold November air, she took a moment to savor the warmth before looking around, as though she sought someone.

Before he could stop himself, Burke stood and waved to get her attention. At first, she gave him a befuddled look before recognition lit her features and she smiled, heading his way.

"If it isn't Officer Tipton. I thought I only ran into you when I literally ran into you," she said in a teasing tone.

Burke chuckled. "Bear and I have kept an eye out for you, but I haven't seen you downtown for a while." Ellen appeared even more beautiful than he remembered. When she unfastened the top buttons of her coat, he gaped at the red and green striped scarf she wore.

"What?" she asked, glancing down as she finished unbuttoning her coat, trying to see what had caught his attention.

"Your scarf," he said, pointing to it. "Please tell me you have a cousin named Liam who set you up on a blind date tonight."

Ellen gawked at him. "You're his friend Tip?"

Burke nodded.

Ellen blinked twice, absorbing this bit of welcome news before draping her coat over a chair. Burke pulled out a seat for her and she sank onto it. When her cousin insisted she go out with his friend weeks ago, Ellen resisted. Liam just wouldn't let the idea go and when he begged her to go out with the guy Friday night, she finally relented. She'd heard him sing the praises of his friend Tip for a long time, but had never met the man. Not that she and Liam spent a lot of time hanging out together, but neither of them had any siblings. Liam had always watched out for her and she'd enjoyed playing the role of his younger sister.

She'd thought it odd he demanded she wear a ridiculous green and red scarf her aunt had made for her a few years ago, but she'd wrapped it around her neck and headed out the door. Although she had no clue what her date looked like, Liam assured her the scarf would be how the mystery man identified her.

Liam had told her to be at the pizza place by half past six, completely aware she'd show up at least fifteen minutes early. Ellen would have been there even sooner, but she'd stopped to help a neighbor who was trying to get two crying children and a car full of groceries packed into her apartment.

"Tip?" Ellen asked, yanking off the scarf and tossing it over her coat. "Why does my well-meaning, intruding, scheming cousin call you Tip?"

Burke took a seat across the table from Ellen and leaned back. He'd have to do something extra nice for his friend. Liam had listened as Burke talked about a young attorney running into him and Bear not once but twice and had pumped him for more details. When Burke shared her name, Liam didn't show any outward recognition, but apparently he'd been scheming all along to get the two of them together.

"Most of my friends call me Tip. Short for Tipton," he said, inordinately pleased to have Ellen as his date. He'd thought of her often the last month, wondering how she was doing and what she'd do if he suddenly showed up at her apartment and asked her for a date. Afraid of freaking her out, he'd refrained, but his interest in her remained.

"Well, Tip, of all the hairbrained, crazy things Liam has talked me into this has definitely got to be the best yet. I may even have to forgive him for his trickery and subterfuge." Ellen leaned forward and dropped her voice slightly. "I told him about a police officer and his horse trying to bring about my demise. Liam never said a word about knowing who you were."

"He didn't say anything to me either when I told him a hotshot attorney was so busy plotting her next step up the corporate ladder, she couldn't pay attention to a large horse blocking her path." Burke's warm smile softened his words. "I'm really glad EJ turned out to be you. I get the Ellen part of that, obviously. What's the J stand for?"

"Juliet. My mother was big into the classics around the time I was born." Ellen spoke in a conspiratorial tone. "It's ridiculous, I know, but I'm stuck with it anyway."

Burke reached down beside him and lifted a single coral-hued rose. He handed it to Ellen with a rascally grin. "In that case, 'That which we call a rose by any other word would smell as sweet,' oh lovely, Juliet." He waggled an eyebrow at her, hoping his ability to quote Shakespeare left her a little impressed.

Shocked by the flower and Burke's quoting Shakespeare, Ellen took the rose and buried her nose in the bloom. She somehow doubted Burke knew the shade of blossom he chose represented desire, but the thought of it made her cheeks flood with color.

"Thank you, Burke. This is lovely," she said, sniffing it again before setting it down on the table beside her. "It's a beautiful color."

"I'll confess I had a little help from my sister. I had no idea what color to choose and Bella assured me that one was perfect for a blind date." He grinned. "If I didn't like the date, I was going to leave it sitting right there on the chair."

Burke gave her a look that appeared so innocent of the rose's true meaning, Ellen tamped down her humor. She had an idea his sister meant to have a little fun at his expense.

After a server came and took their order, Burke leaned back and draped an arm over the chair next to him in a relaxed pose. "There's something different about you, Ellen. I noticed it the last time you barreled into me and Sugar Bear. Is everything okay?"

"Actually, life is very good, Burke." Ellen leaned forward again and clasped his hand between both of hers. Warmth and something electric hummed in her blood at the contact, but she held on, intent on doing what she should have done months ago. "I need to offer you an apology and my thanks."

Puzzled, he remained unmoving, allowing her to sandwich his hand between hers. "For what?"

"The apology is for the two times I ran into you and Sugar Bear. Both times were entirely my fault and I am sorry for being such a blundering klutz."

"You're not a klutz," Burke said. "No one as beautiful and graceful as you could possibly bear that title."

The twinkle in his eyes made something stir in her midsection, but she chose to ignore it. "I am a klutz. If you don't believe me, ask my friend, Tara. At the most inopportune moments, it rears its ugly head."

Burke chuckled softly. "Still not buying it, but you are forgiven. You suffered more from both mishaps than Bear and I did."

Grateful he accepted her apology, she nodded. "Regardless, I did want to apologize." She inhaled a deep breath and continued. "And I want to thank you for changing my life."

Burke leaned closer and moved his hands so they cradled hers. "What are you talking about? How did I change your life?"

"Remember the first time I bumped into you? You were so upset with me for defending Mr. Westmont. You accused me of being just as bad as him for helping him go free."

A stricken look passed over his face. "I'm sorry about that, Ellen. I shouldn't have mouthed off. I was still just so frustrated that all those poor people lost everything and he walked away unpunished."

"No, you were right, Burke," she assured him, unsettled by the feel of his big, warm palms holding hers. She could feel the rough calluses and weathered skin and glanced down at his tanned fingers. His hands were sturdy, with a cut across two knuckles, and showed the fact they were used for hard labor. While some might find them unappealing, she found them incredibly attractive.

A sigh rolled up from her chest before she lifted her gaze to his again. "For longer than I care to admit, I've been focused on climbing the ladder, doing better than my peers, snagging the next promotion. Somewhere along the way, I lost sight of why I wanted to become an attorney — so I could help people. What you said made me angry, so angry."

At his surprised expression, she grinned at him. "I may have muttered a few unkind things about you as I marched up to my client's office. But by the time I left that appointment, both my head and heart were convicted by what you said. The next day, I gave my two-week's notice at work and started looking for a new job."

"You're pulling my leg," Burke said, glancing at her in confusion. "You're thanking me because I gave you a case of guilt that made you quit your job?"

"No, that's not what I meant." She took a quick moment to gather her thoughts then raised her gaze back to Burke's. It was hard to concentrate on what she wanted to say with the enticing warmth of his eyes drawing her into a place she knew was pointless to venture. "What I'm trying to say, Burke, is that thanks to you, to what you said, I realized how far I'd strayed off the right path for me. Since August, I've been working in an office that primarily does estate planning and wills, that sort of thing. It might not be glamorous, high-profile work, but it's satisfying and helpful to my clients without being harmful to others. Best of all, I can sleep at night without a guilty conscience keeping me awake. And that is all thanks to you. So thank you for helping me see the error of my ways, even if I wanted to smack the smirk off your face the day you said it."

Burke shot her that very smirk. "I'm glad you didn't because I would have had to arrest you, and that definitely would have put a damper on things." He squeezed her hands. "I'm proud of you, Ellen. It's hard to admit we might be wrong, or pursuing the wrong path. I know from experience it's challenging. But I'm proud of you for following your heart. I'm glad I played a part in it, no matter how small or insignificant."

"Oh, it was a very significant part, Burke. If you hadn't been so forthcoming with your opinions that day, I might still be talking myself into doing things I knew were wrong and growing more miserable by the day." She offered him a smile full of gratitude. "And because I'm no longer trying to scale that lofty ladder of success, I have time to do things I enjoy."

"Like what?" he asked, releasing her hands as their pizza arrived. He served her a piece then slid a slice on his own plate. "What sort of things do you enjoy?"

"Well, I've started volunteering twice a week at a homeless shelter. That's been so fulfilling and rewarding, and a little heartbreaking. It's so hard to see people suffering and struggling, you know?"

"I do know, all too well," Burke said.

"That was stupid of me," Ellen said, blushing. "Of course you see all sorts of terrible things in your work."

Reluctantly, Burke nodded. "Not as much now that I'm with the mounted patrol. It's mostly petty theft, public intoxication, vandalism, and that sort of thing, although I did almost arrest a girl for assaulting two officers a while back." He tossed her a rakish grin. "But one look in her amazing eyes and I couldn't quite slap the cuffs on her."

Ellen stopped mid bite and straightened, not quite convinced Burke referred to her. "What color were the amazing eyes? Blue? Green?"

Burke shook his head and fused his gaze to hers. "No, they're brown, like the finest whiskey."

Her cheeks once again suffused with bright pink color, but she held his gaze. "Drink a lot of whiskey, do you?"

"No, ma'am, I do not. I don't make it a habit to drink a lot of anything except good old water and admittedly more Dr. Pepper than I should. A sergeant

I used to work with thought whiskey was the cure for everything. When he retired, we all chipped in and bought him a bottle of high-dollar stuff." Burke smiled at her again. "And the color was the exact shade of your eyes."

Ellen dropped her eyes to her half-eaten slice of pizza, uncertain if he meant it as a compliment. She'd never been a flirt, hadn't dated many boys, always too focused on her career. "Is that a good thing?"

"A very good thing, Ellen."

As they ate their pizza, Ellen learned Burke had grown up on a ranch in Eastern Oregon with two older brothers and a younger sister. In turn, she shared about having no siblings, but managed to survive the dreaded teen years with her best friend at her side.

"It's so hard not having Tara around. She and I were inseparable from the time we were eleven until she left for Atlanta last year." Unknowingly, she released a heavy sigh. "I miss her."

Aware of her melancholy, Burke decided she had to be closer to Tara than he was to his own brothers. He'd been nothing but eager to get away from their joking, tormenting presences. "Do you talk to her often?"

Ellen looked up at him with a sad smile. "I do. We usually text at least once a day and talk on Sunday evenings. She and Brett are expecting their first baby in January, so I imagine after the little one arrives, she'll have even less time to stay in touch."

"Why don't you go visit her? I'm sure she'd welcome your company. Don't new mothers need a lot of help?"

Taken aback by his suggestion and his insight into what she wanted to do, Ellen grinned. "They do and I've been thinking about going to visit her once her mother returns from her visit as the doting grandmother. Besides, I haven't been at my new job long enough to have built up much time off." She straightened and looked around the busy restaurant. The packed tables made the noise level so loud, it had become hard to talk without shouting.

Burke must have noticed the same thing. "Want to get out of here? The Friday crowd is usually a little loud and boisterous."

"Sure," Ellen said, picking up her scarf and winding it around her neck while Burke tugged on his coat and lifted a cowboy hat from the chair beside his.

Ellen stopped fussing with her scarf and watched him settle it on his dark head, entranced.

When she finally regained her senses and stood, Burke was beside her, holding her coat as she slipped her arms in the sleeves. He stayed close as they made their way around the tables to the front counter. She started to dig into her purse to pay for her share, but Burke tossed cash to the girl along with his receipt and tipped his hat to her.

Ellen giggled as they stepped outside into the chilly evening air. "I should have known."

"Known what?" Burke asked as he lightly settled his hand against Ellen's back and shortened his stride to match hers.

"You're a cowboy."

Chapter Four

Burke winked at her and spoke with a thick western twang as he took a few swaggering steps. "I shore 'nuff am, ma'am. Since we've dun already wrangled up some vittles, I'd be right pleased to show ya a real good time."

Her giggles turned to full-out laughter and she stopped, casting him a sideways glance. "I noticed your twang the first time we met, although this one is way over the top."

"Twang?" Burke's brow puckered as he spoke in his regular voice. "What twang?"

"Oh, I don't know how to explain it. You just have a hint of a twang or drawl when you speak, but that seems strange since you're from Oregon, not Texas."

Burke dropped his hand from her back, stuffing both hands inside the pockets of his jacket. "I've been accused of having a twang before, mostly when I was in college. One of my professors called it a 'rural dialect' although I'm not sure he meant it in a good way." He shrugged. "Most of the people I know back home talk just like I do. Despite what you might think, we aren't all a bunch of uneducated rednecks."

Ellen stopped and placed a hand on his arm. "I didn't mean to imply anything negative with the comment, Burke. I like it. It makes you sound… different." She couldn't very well tell him she could listen to him speak for hours, even reciting the alphabet, because she loved his voice, not just the sexy little twang, but the deep richness of it, too.

"Is different a good thing?"

"Very good," she smiled and wrapped both hands around his arm, unsettled by the rock hard bicep her fingers encircled. "Unless you plan to freeze in the rain that's about to begin falling in earnest, I think we should go."

Burke studied her hands as they rested on his arm for a moment before looking back at her face. "Would you mind going for a little drive?"

"Not at all. I walked from my apartment. If we head back there…" Ellen released his arm and turned in the direction they'd come.

Burke caught her hand in his and pulled her back around. "My pickup is parked right over there. Let's go."

He held the passenger door for her and gave her a hand into his pickup. Much to her surprise, the inside was clean and smelled of Burke — like sunshine mixed with leather and a hint of longing. She inhaled, filling her nose with the delicious scent as she fastened her seatbelt.

"So, where are we headed?" she asked as he slid behind the wheel and backed out of the parking space then pulled onto the street.

"There's someone I'd like you to meet," he said, looking at her then focusing on the street.

"You want me to meet someone?" Ellen nervously toyed with her scarf. What if it was a family member? His best friend? Who wanted to make introductions like that on a first date? Maybe she should feign a headache and ask Burke to take her home.

One glance at him, though, and her apprehension settled. Burke was safety and security personified. He wouldn't do anything to frighten or harm her. Instinctively, she knew that to be true.

He grinned at her again, his teeth flashing white in the shadowed darkness of the pickup cab as he pulled onto the freeway. "I do want you to meet someone. I think you'll like it. Just trust me."

"Famous last words." Ellen leaned back and relaxed. "You wouldn't believe how many times Tara uttered those words to me right before we ended up in a bunch of trouble."

Burke lifted a dark eyebrow. "So you were the good girl and your wayward friend dragged you into trouble. You never instigated any of it?"

"Well..." Ellen couldn't hold back a sheepish look. "I probably could be blamed for at least half the trouble we got into."

"Now the truth comes out," Burke said, exiting the freeway. He drove at a snail's pace past a truck stop, craning his neck to look at something before he sped up and continued on his way. A few miles later, he turned on a side street, then another and drove to the last house on a dead-end street filled with modest yet tidy homes. He pulled into the driveway and turned off the lights. "Home, sweet home."

Any number of red flags snapped to attention in Ellen's mind as Burke hurried around the pickup to help her out. Was he some crazy cavedweller, planning to lock her in his house and have his way with her? Was he a cop by day and a serial killer by night? What if there wasn't anyone he wanted her to meet and it was all a ruse to get her to his place? What if…

Ellen looked into his handsome, honest face and released her fears. Burke was one of the good guys. At least she thought he was.

"Come on," he said, taking her hand and leading her across the sidewalk to the front door. After he opened it, he flicked on a switch and soft light bathed his living room.

Hesitantly, Ellen stepped inside and looked around. Burke's dark brown and pine wood furnishings gave the place a definite masculine feel. Black and white images of horses and ranch scenes graced one wall while a big screen TV took up much of another.

The place was as neat and tidy as his pickup and smelled wonderfully like Burke.

"It's nice," she said, stepping further inside.

He gave her a look that said he knew she was only being polite. "It's in a decent neighborhood, and the rent's reasonable, but the reason I rent this place is for the yard."

"The yard?" Ellen asked as he led the way into the kitchen where the light over the stove offered a small swath of light.

Lights illuminated the room with the click of another switch. They moved through the kitchen to a small utility room. Burke turned on the overhead light then unlocked the back door and pulled it open. "The backyard is almost half an acre. It gives Lovey plenty of room to play when I'm not home."

"Lovey?" Ellen watched as a blur of red and white fur shot out of a doghouse across the yard, and slid to a stop at Burke's feet.

He hunkered down and rubbed an affectionate hand over the soft fur of the red Border collie. "Ellen, I'd like you to meet Lovey. Lovey this beautiful woman is Miss Ellen Meade. Can you tell her hello, girl?"

The dog lifted one paw to Ellen, as though she wanted to shake hands. Delighted, Ellen bent down and shook the dog's paw then gently ran a hand over the dog's head and scratched behind Lovey's ears. Her efforts were rewarded with an enthusiastic lick to her chin.

"She's gorgeous, Burke. What a pretty girl," Ellen crooned to the dog, cupping her chin and making note of the dog's pale blue eyes. "Yes, you are Lovey. You are a very pretty girl."

The dog wagged her backend and her ears perked up, as though she greatly appreciated the compliment.

"Let's get you inside out of the cold," Burke said as he straightened.

At first, Ellen assumed he spoke to the dog. When he took her elbow in his hand and smiled down at her, she realized he meant her. Warmed by his attention and care, she followed him inside. Lovey dashed in front of them, her feet skidding on the linoleum of the floor. She turned in a circle and yipped excitedly, her focus dancing between Burke and a large jar on a shelf above the washing machine.

"Lovey, you know better than to beg," Burke cautioned the canine. Lovey sat back on her haunches and appeared to pout.

Ellen had to look away, lest she laugh at the scene of the cowboy bent over the sulking dog. He whispered something to the dog and took several steps back. "Okay, Lovey, circle time."

The dog yipped once more then raced to Burke, leaping up as she neared him. He held out his hands, like a step. The dog used them to give herself a push and flipped over in a circle before he caught her in his arms.

Lovey barked, as though calling attention to her superb skills, and then licked Burke's neck.

Spontaneously, Ellen clapped, thoroughly enchanted by the dog and her owner. "Oh, that was unbelievable!"

Burke handed Lovey a treat from the jar then set her down on the floor. She wagged her tail then trotted over to a food bowl and began crunching away on her dinner.

"Take a bow, Lovey," Burke commanded.

The dog turned away from her food, stretched out her left leg in front of her then touched her nose to the extended to leg.

"Oh, my gracious, Burke! She is fantastic!" Ellen gushed, rubbing a hand over the dog's head before Lovey returned to her food.

"She is pretty special. Once she eats her fill, she'll wander into the front room to visit," Burke said, guiding Ellen back to the living room. He helped her out of her coat and tossed it over a side chair then removed his coat and hat, leaving them on the chair with hers.

"Would you like something to drink? I have soda pop, juice, and milk. I may even have some tea left over from the last time Bella came to visit." Burke took a step toward the kitchen.

"Tea sounds wonderful, but I can help with it." Ellen followed him back to the kitchen.

He set out the tea and sugar then filled a mug with water and set it in the microwave. While they waited for it to heat, Ellen went back to the utility room door to watch Lovey. She turned to Burke with such a soft look on her face that he almost dropped the mug before he set it on the counter and scooted it toward her.

"How long have you had Lovey?" Ellen asked as she dropped a tea bag into the mug and waited for it to steep.

"Since she was about eight weeks old. I was at the ranch for a weekend visit when one of our neighbors stopped by and mentioned he had a few pups he wanted to get rid of. I went over there and Lovey decided she wanted to come home with me. Of course, I had an apartment then that didn't allow pets. I had to smuggle her in and immediately began looking for a place that would give her a big yard to play in." Burke edged a bowl of sugar closer to Ellen. "This place isn't fancy, by any means, but she has plenty of room for playing. I traded installing the fence for rent. I've done some improvements around here and the landlord is good about taking the cost of both my labor and supplies off the rent. I think he likes having an officer in this neighborhood, because he owns three other houses around here. He claims it cuts down on the riffraff."

Ellen pointed her spoon in the direction of the dog. "Did you teach her all those tricks?"

"I did. It gave me something to do in my free time besides sitting around bored. Lovey keeps things from being too quiet or lonely around here."

"You're very fortunate to have her, Burke, and she's very lucky to have you."

He tipped his head toward her with a pleased smile. "Why, thank you, kind lady."

She took a sip of her tea and rolled her eyes. "Oh, my word. That is delicious. I may need to buy a box of this. What is it?"

"I don't know, just some stuff my sister brought when she was here a few weekends ago." Burke held the box of tea out to Ellen. "You can keep it if you want."

"No, I wouldn't think of stealing Bella's tea, but I will get some of my own." She took her phone from her pocket and snapped a photo of the box, so she wouldn't forget the name or brand. "It tastes like Christmas and happy memories."

Burke shook his head at her fanciful description, but smiled indulgently. "Let's go sit somewhere comfortable." He snagged a bottle of soda pop from the fridge then guided Ellen back into the living room. They both sat on the couch, on opposite ends. For a moment, the only sound was the effervescent whistle of carbonated bubbles as he unscrewed the cap on his Dr. Pepper.

"Do you often…"

"Have you ever…"

They spoke at the same time, looked at each other and laughed, breaking the uncomfortable silence.

"Go ahead, Ellen," Burke said, pointing toward her with the bottle of pop. "What did you start to say?"

"I was just going to ask if your sister comes to visit you often. I get the idea the two of you are close."

Burke took a swig of his drink then leaned back against the soft cushions of the couch. "Despite our age difference, we are close."

"How old is Bella?" Ellen asked, then took another dainty sip of her tea.

"The little brat is twenty-one. I was seven when she was born. Although I'm closer in age to my brothers, Bella and I have always gotten along well." Burke grinned. "When she gets tired of college life, she comes and spends the weekend with me, dragging along all her laundry. In exchange for me putting up with her for the weekend, she cooks the meals, but only if I fill her detailed grocery lists."

"Sounds like a great compromise," Ellen said, wondering what it would be like to have a sibling, especially one like Burke. She could envision him as the perfect older brother, one who was protective and supportive without being smothering.

A clicking sound of nails on linoleum preceded the dog as she raced through the kitchen. Lovey ran into the living room and wiggled to a stop at Burke's feet.

SHANNA HATFIELD

"Did you have a good dinner, Lovey?" Burke asked, rubbing a hand over the dog's head.

Lovey waggled her entire body while her tongue lapped at his hand.

He glanced over at Ellen. "I leave her food and water outside, since I never know when I'll be home, but she much prefers to eat inside." He looked back at the dog. "Don't you, girl? You're just another persnickety female, aren't you?"

Ellen cleared her throat in warning. "I suggest you not make such broad, expansive statements, Officer Tipton. They might get you into trouble."

He winked at her. "Nah. Lovey knows I'm only teasing." Before Ellen could work up a proper protest, Burke reached out to her. "Lovey loves attention. You can scoot closer if you'd like to pet her."

Ellen took one more sip from her nearly empty mug then set it on the coffee table before sliding closer to Burke. The warmth of his body combined with his luscious scent wrapped her in a comforting embrace in spite of the fact he kept one hand on the dog and the other holding his drink.

"Did Bella name the dog, too?" Ellen asked as she held a hand down for Lovey to sniff.

"No. You can blame that on my mom. When I brought the puppy home from the neighbor's place, mom cuddled her for awhile and declared her to be such a little love, that the name just sort of stuck. So she's Lovey." He rubbed a hand along the dog's side. "Aren't you, girl. You're my sweet little Lovey."

The dog nuzzled his hand and leaned against his leg then licked Ellen's fingers.

48

"She is sweet, Burke." Ellen leaned down and rubbed both hands over the dog's head. Lovey flopped onto the floor and rolled onto her back. Ellen obliged by scratching her tummy while the dog sighed in bliss.

"You may not realize it, but you'll be considered one of her friends for life now. There is nothing she likes better than having her stomach rubbed unless it's herding something."

"Herding something?" Ellen asked, continuing to scratch the dog's belly. Lovey's leg twitched with each scratch, making Ellen hold back a giggle.

"Lovey is a Border collie. Herding livestock is in their blood. Although, when I take her to the park, she's perfectly happy trying to herd the ducks. Once, she even herded a group of kids away from a homeless guy who was sleeping on a bench and having a nightmare."

"Oh, wow! That is incredible."

Ellen gave Lovey one last scratch then leaned back. While the dog slept at their feet, they just talked. And talked. And talked. They spoke of family, college, jobs, favorite things, their top dislikes, and dreams.

In all her twenty-six years, she'd never felt so comfortable around a man, particularly not one so fun, funny, and handsome.

When Ellen yawned, Burke glanced at the clock across the room and jumped to his feet. "I'm so sorry, Ellen. I didn't mean to keep you out this late."

Shocked to see the time, she rose and followed him to the door. "I had no idea it was nearly morning,

Burke. I'm sorry I kept you up all night. Do you have to work tomorrow? Or is that today?"

Softly, he chuckled and reached for her coat, then glanced back at her. "As late as it is, you want to just crash here for a while?"

Caught off guard by his question, her eyes widened. "Burke, I'm not… I don't…"

He held up his hands, as if he wanted to placate her. "I just meant to sleep a while. I have a guest room. Bella always makes sure it's ready when she leaves."

"Oh, I…" Ellen felt her cheeks burn with embarrassment. "If you don't mind driving me, I think it's probably best I go home. I could always call a cab."

"No. I'll take you. Just let me chase Lovey outside and I'll be right back." Burke walked to the kitchen and whistled twice.

The dog awakened from her bed near what had to be Burke's recliner and scrambled into the kitchen.

Ellen heard Burke praising the dog before he shooed her outside and locked the back door. He soon reappeared and hurried to pull on his coat and settle a hat on his head.

"Let's get you home," he said, placing his hand on her back as they walked outside in the cold, drizzly weather.

Ellen started to shiver before the heat kicked on in Burke's pickup. He lifted one of her hands in his and raised it to his lips, blowing warm air across her skin. Immediately, she forgot about being cold, tired, or late getting home. Warmth unlike anything she'd ever experienced flooded through her like a river overflowing its banks. Harsh, unexpected, frightening and powerful — emotions simmered, senses engaged, nerves spiked until all she could think about was how marvelous it felt to have Burke hold her hand. He moved it from his lips to rest clasped with his on his hard thigh as he drove her home.

In the illumination from the streetlights, she studied his profile, wondered if he'd be offended if she thought him beautiful. Oh, he was rugged and masculine, but a master sculptor could have carved his profile. The lines were perfection from the sweep of his brow, the thick eyelashes, the straight form of his nose, the curve of his lips, to the firm square jaw.

As they drove past the truck stop, Burke once again slowed down and looked observantly out the window.

"What is it?" she asked, breaking the comfortable silence between them.

"Nothing," he said, absently.

Ellen leaned closer and nudged his side with her elbow. "I'm an attorney. I know when someone is being evasive. It's not 'nothing.' Something out there has you concerned. What is it?"

He gave her a questioning glance then tipped his head toward the parking lot. "You see that old beat-up car parked close to the convenience store?"

At her nod, he continued. "It's been parked in that same spot the last four days. Three times, I've seen a little kid getting in and out of it. Just makes me wonder what's going on. If it's still there Monday, I think I'll stop and check things out."

"Just be careful, Burke," Ellen said, feeling oddly protective of him.

Burke grinned at her and squeezed her hand. "Oh, don't you worry, darlin'. I'm always careful."

It didn't take long for him to reach her apartment. He not only walked her inside the building but insisted on seeing her up to her door.

As she unlocked it and flicked on the light, Burke leaned one arm against the doorjamb, watching her.

Nervous under his scrutiny, she fumbled with the keys and dropped them on her tiled entry with a loud clang.

Quickly snatching them up, she stepped inside and set them on the table by the door. "I'd ask you to come in, but I'm sure you're exhausted. Will you be okay driving yourself home?"

"Absolutely." Burke didn't make any move to leave.

Instead, his slow, lazy grin made her want to press her mouth to his and savor a lingering kiss. Her mouth flooded with moisture but she forced herself to a take a step back.

"Thank you for a lovely evening, Burke," she said, lowering her voice to a whisper. "It was the nicest blind date, or first date, I've ever had."

His grin broadened. "If you're calling it a first date that must mean you're willing for a second."

"I just might be." Ellen returned his smile. "Do you have something in mind?"

"Not yet, but how about I think of something and give you a call?"

Ellen nodded her head. "That would be perfect, except you'll need my number."

"Right," Burke said, pulling his cell phone from his pocket and entering her number then sending her a text so she'd have his. He backed away, still smiling at her. "Thank you for a great evening, Ellen. I'm really glad EJ turned out to be you."

"I'm glad Tip was you," Ellen said, watching him back down the hall. "Thanks again, Burke."

He nodded and touched his fingers to the brim of his hat then turned away. Ellen dropped her gaze for a moment, feeling bereft from his presence after spending so much time together that evening. Disappointment clawed at her that he hadn't so much as pecked her cheek.

With a sigh, she took a step back to close the door and found herself hauled against a solid, muscled chest.

"I've already broken every first date or blind date rule, so what the heck," Burke muttered as his lips took possession of hers.

The kiss was as far from a friendly peck as Ellen had ever experienced. In fact, it was the most tantalizing, spellbinding, and thorough kiss she'd ever received.

Knees weak and heart racing, she clasped the collar of Burke's coat for support as his lips moved against hers, sending bright sparks of passion firing through her entire body.

Just when she thought she would lose the ability to hold herself upright, Burke raised his head and released his hold. He lifted one hand, his thumb grazing across her puffy, just-kissed lips.

"You're even sweeter than I imagined, Miss Ellen Juliet Meade." With a rascally wink, he backed away from her once again. "'Good night, good night! Parting is such sweet sorrow that I shall say good night till it be morrow.'" He doffed his hat with an exaggerated flourish then jogged along the hall and disappeared down the stairs.

Ellen closed her door and leaned against it, sliding down until she sat on the floor, wondering if she'd ever recover from being kissed by Officer-Hunkalicious.

Chapter Five

"He's just so…" Ellen sighed languorously and flopped back on her bed, holding her cell phone to her ear.

"So what?" Tara Cutler asked.

Ellen didn't know how to explain to her best friend that the officer she'd whined about being mean to her last summer had charmed her so thoroughly, she'd spent the entire weekend wishing he'd show up at her door and kiss her again.

"So… delicious," Ellen said, then broke into giggles that Tara echoed.

"Tell me more about this hunky hottie police officer who turned out to be a real life cowboy. How he has redeemed himself from the, and I quote you, El, 'insufferable, overbearing, miscreant in need of anger management classes,' to a man who makes you flop back on your bed and sigh dreamily?"

Ellen sat up. "How did you know I'm on my bed and sighing dreamily? Did you install cameras when you and Brett came to visit?"

"No, you weirdo!" Tara laughed. "But I know you, Ellen. For the record, Burke sounds like a great guy and I'm glad you've finally gotten to the place in your life where you're willing to be a little adventurous. You know, not everything has to follow that detailed plan you have for your life."

"Oh, that," Ellen said, sobering. "You'll be happy to know I ran that plan through the shredder a while back. Look what it did to me. Almost turned me into one of those horrible people who only cares about their career and not the people they hurt in achieving their goals. I'm done with all that."

"And I'm so glad to hear that you are. For a while, I worried about you selling your soul to the devil, or at least your horrible boss." Tara's voice softened. "Are you sure you're doing okay, El? It was a big change to go from cutthroat attorney to helping people plan estates and writing living wills."

"I know, but I really do enjoy working with the clients and it leaves me time to actually have a life."

The smile was back in Tara's voice. "I'm so proud of you. Are you still planning to volunteer at the homeless shelter through the holidays?"

"I am. In fact, I'm going to help serve Thanksgiving dinner, although that's actually on Wednesday. Then we'll start working on holiday projects next week. I can't believe Christmas is only a month away."

Tara sighed. "I can't wait for Christmas to come and go because then I'll only be two weeks away from getting my little bun out of the oven."

Ellen rolled her eyes. "Only a pastry chef would refer to the upcoming arrival of her firstborn as removing a bun from the oven. What does Brett say?"

"He can't wait. We've picked out two dozen names, and can't seem to narrow it down to one or two we like. And he's started fussing. His mom said it's as natural as it is annoying, but I'm glad I can still hide out at work for a few more weeks. I'd go crazy if I had him hovering around me twenty-four hours a day."

"Oh, poor little Tara. Her prince charming loves her so much he can't bear to have her out of his sight. What a tragedy." Ellen pressed a hand to her brow in a dramatic gesture although no one could see her.

Tara laughed. "Whatever, smarty. Why don't you put a little more effort into snagging your own prince? Or maybe it's a cowboy you're after?"

Ellen scowled. "I'm not after anyone. For your information…"

Tara's laughter halted her tirade. "I'm just teasing you, El, but you sound so happy when you talk about Officer Tipton. Do you have a photo of him you can share? I want to see him for myself."

"I don't have a photo, yet, but he did ask me for a second date. That's a good sign, right?"

"Absolutely. What did you say you two did after you had pizza Friday night?"

Ellen turned onto her side and propped her head up on her elbow, plying Tara with details from her date.

"What in the world were you doing out with him until four in the morning, Ellen Juliet Meade? Are you nuts? Don't you know all the bad stuff you hear in the news happens after midnight?" Tara said, admonishment heavy in her tone.

Ellen scoffed. "He was a perfect gentleman, Tara. We just got so involved in talking, we lost track of the time. He drove me home, walked me to the door, and bid me good night while quoting Shakespeare."

"And?" Tara asked.

"And what?"

"The kiss, you goose! Did he kiss you or not?"

"Oh, yeah, he did," Ellen admitted then clapped a hand over her mouth.

Tara hooted with laughter. "Well, then, I guess my job here is done, other than to warn you not to do anything you wouldn't do if I was still your roomie. Wait! Scratch that. Definitely do something you wouldn't do then because all you did was work. Have fun. Take a chance. Fall in love."

"You are crazy, Tara."

"Crazy for my horse-wrangling hubby, but you already knew that." Tara spoke to someone in the background then came back on the line. "I need to run, El, but promise me you'll give Officer Tipton a chance. He really does sound like a good person. I mean, where else are you going to find a good-looking guy who rides a horse to work, quotes Shakespeare, and has an adorable dog? As Rhett Butler would say, you need to be kissed, and often, by a hunky cowboy cop who knows how. If Officer Tipton knows how, let 'em at those lips of yours!"

"Goodbye, Tara!" Ellen disconnected the call on a laugh, amused by her friend. As teens, and even up until Tara left to pursue her dreams in the South, the two girls could recite entire passages of *Gone With the Wind* by heart. Tara's husband, the dashing Brett Cutler (and every time Ellen thought of how much his name sounded like Rhett Butler, she giggled), had swept her off her feet in their own version of a sweet romance. For Tara it might have been all sweet tea and kisses, but she'd fallen hard for Brett from the moment they met.

Ellen wasn't convinced she'd ever find a hero that fulfilled the lofty dreams she'd cultivated since she was old enough to know what romance meant. It would take someone special to fill those imaginary shoes, or boots, as the case may be.

With nothing else to occupy her time, she picked up the book she'd been reading, a fun romance about a mechanic from Portland who ended up on a ranch in the middle of nowhere, and lost herself in the world of someone else's love story for a while.

Chapter Six

Burke drove past the truck stop, slowing so he could scan the parking lot. The car he'd been keeping an eye on was back. It had disappeared the weekend he'd gone on the date with Ellen and he thought perhaps whoever was squatting in it had moved on.

Thanksgiving had come and gone, and now, on the first of December, it appeared the car was back. At first, he'd thought the car was red with some faded white streaks on it. Upon closer examination, he'd realized the car wasn't red, but rusted. It boggled his mind how the thing continued to run let alone travel down the road without leaving large chunks of the body behind.

He clicked on his turn signal and pulled into the truck stop, parking in front of a gas pump. While the attendant fueled up his pickup, he covertly studied the car. He could see movement in it, but not enough he was convinced it was an adult.

Once his tank was full, he took the receipt and offered the attendant a word of thanks before he drove over to the rusted old heap. The Cadillac might have been nice when it rolled off the assembly line back in the early seventies, but the long, long length of it, along with the deplorable condition made it nothing more than an eyesore.

Burke parked a few parking spaces away from the car and got out of his pickup. With easy strides, he walked past the car, appearing as though he wanted nothing more than to run inside the convenience store.

He purchased a cup of hot chocolate and looked to see if the manager was around. After spying the man restocking a shelf full of motor oil, Burke made his way over to him.

"Hey, Paul, do you know anything about that old wreck parked outside?" Burke jutted his chin in the direction of the car.

The manager straightened his back and sighed. "I gave the guy driving it permission to park it there. He's down on his luck, but he's pretty closedmouthed about his story. He has a kid with him, but other than that, I don't know much. The kid didn't act scared of him, like she's kidnapped or anything, or I would have called you the last time he parked here."

"How long has he been hanging around here?" Burke asked.

Paul rubbed a finger alongside his nose, digging through his memory for details. "First time he showed up was back in October. He only stayed a few days that time. The second time was in November. He parked here for almost two weeks. Then he showed up yesterday. The guy didn't look good at all, like he's sick or something. I haven't seen him get out of the car today, but I did see the kid. She came in to use the restroom a little while ago."

Burke shook the man's hand. "Thanks for the info, Paul. I appreciate it."

"Don't go arresting the kid, okay? She looks like she's had a tough time of it."

"I don't arrest kids, only criminals." Burke nodded to the manager and made his way outside.

He made a beeline for the car and stopped only when he stood next to the driver's window.

A little girl snuggled beneath a snowflake-patterned fleece blanket on the front seat with a storybook held in red mitten-covered hands. A matching red stocking cap adorned her head. An unconscious man with a blanket pulled up to his waist occupied the backseat. Even through the water-stained, wavy glass, Burke could see the man didn't look well.

Raising his hand, he tapped on the glass, drawing a startled shriek from the child although the man in the backseat didn't stir.

"Open the door, please," Burke said, motioning to the handle.

The child shook her head, big green eyes wide with fright.

Burke bent down and pointed to the police emblem on the front of his coat. "My name is Officer Tipton. I just want to check on your dad, honey. Will you please unlock the door?"

"How do I know you're really a cop?" the child asked, eyeing him speculatively as she crawled on her knees over to the driver's side of the car and placed both hands over the lock, as though that single action would keep him out.

"I have a badge," Burke said, showing it to her.

"You could have bought that online." The little imp glared at him through the window. "If you're really a cop, what's your partner's name?"

Burke grinned. "Sugar Bear. I'm part of the Mounted Patrol Unit. My partner is a horse, a handsome red one."

At her dubious expression, Burke whipped out his phone, hastily scrolled through the photographs, and showed her a photo of him standing next to Sugar Bear.

Her little rosebud lips formed a perfect O as she studied the photo. Finally, she let her hands slide down to her lap. "Do you really ride a horse? Every day?"

"Every day that I work and sometimes just for fun when I don't. Do you like horses?" Burke was about ready to break his way into the car, but he didn't want to upset the child. Despite the fact she was living in a car and had to be just a step above freezing, she possessed a lot of spunk.

"I love horses." A gap-toothed smile where her front teeth were missing added to her charm as she reached to unlock the door. She hesitated and tossed him a narrowed glare that almost made him laugh. "If you try anything funny, mister, my daddy gave me a can of mace and showed me how to use it."

Burke held up both hands, although one held the rapidly cooling cup of hot chocolate. "I promise I just want to check on your dad, honey. He looks like he could use some help."

She unlocked the door and scrambled back out of Burke's way. He reached inside and unlocked the back door. The car was as cold inside as the weather outside.

"Here, will you take this hot chocolate for me? I bought it then remembered I don't want to spoil my dinner." He handed the child the cup. "Go on and drink it if you want. I'll just have to throw it away if you don't."

In spite of her efforts to hide her enthusiasm over the warm drink, the child's green eyes glittered like twin emeralds as she took a careful sip, finding the temperature just right.

Burke smiled at her then opened the door to the backseat. He felt the man's pulse in his neck. The child's father was still alive, but barely. He stepped back from the car and placed a call, requesting an ambulance and alerting the sheriff's office since the truck stop was out of city jurisdiction.

He leaned back into the car and pulled the blanket further up on the man's inert form. "How long has your daddy been sick?" he asked the child. She stood on the seat, drinking the hot chocolate and watching his every move.

"Since Thanksgiving. We had a nice dinner at a warm place with lots of people. Daddy said he didn't feel good that night and he was sick the next day." Tears glistened in her eyes. "Will my dad be okay?"

"Sure, honey, but he needs to see a doctor."

Fear filled her face. She set the hot chocolate on the dash and reached out to grasp Burke's arm with both hands. "Please don't let them take Daddy. Please! You can't let them take my daddy away. Doctors are bad."

"It's okay, honey. It's okay," Burke said, placing his hand over both hers where they rested on his arm. "What's your dad's name?"

"John Hayes."

"That's a fine name." Burke smiled at her, hoping to keep her calm. "What's your name?"

"Missy," the girl said, not taking her eyes from Burke's face.

"Well, Missy, I promise the doctors your dad will see aren't bad. They'll help him get well. Do you have someone you can stay with until your dad is all better?"

The tiny head slowly moved from left to right in an almost unnoticeable shake of denial.

"How about your mom? Where's she?" Burke asked, moving from the backseat and hunkering down in the open front door so he didn't tower over the child.

Missy's bottom lip began to quiver and the tears that had pricked at her eyes rolled down her cheeks. "Dead. Mommy died right after Easter."

"Aw, Missy. I'm sorry." Burke reached out to the child.

She leaned away from him and gave him a long, questioning look before she swiped at her tears with the backs of her mitten-covered hands.

"How about grandparents?"

A shake of her head.

"Aunts? Uncles? Siblings? Cousins?"

Another shake.

"Did your parents have any close friends?"

"Not really. Our friends moved away last year, before Christmas. Then Mommy got sick. The doctors couldn't fix her. They said the cancer was advanced, whatever that means. The doctors wanted to keep her in the hospital all hooked up to tubes and scary stuff, but Daddy brought her home and we took care of her until she…" Missy gulped and scrubbed her eyes again. "Until Mommy died."

"Does your dad have a job?" Burke could hear the sirens of the ambulance, but didn't lift his gaze from the frightened child.

"No. He quit his job to take care of Mommy. After she died, they wouldn't take him back. He's been trying to find a new job. We had to sell our house to pay the doctor's bills. We had to sell my pretty bed and my toys, and even our table and fridge. Then Daddy sold his car and Mommy's minivan and bought this car." Her nose wrinkled in revulsion.

"And you've been living in this car for a while?"

Missy nodded. "Since before Halloween."

"Do you go to school?"

"Sometimes. Daddy takes me to school and picks me up when he's not sick." Missy sniffled and pulled a paper napkin out of her pocket, wiping her nose on the rough surface.

"How old are you, Missy?" Burke asked, watching the ambulance pull into the parking lot. He stood and waved to them.

"I'm almost seven. My birthday is Christmas Day." At the sight of the ambulance, she shrieked and launched her small body over the seat and threw herself against her father, clinging to his coat. "Don't take my daddy to the hospital! They'll kill him! They'll kill him just like they did Mommy! No!"

Her wails ripped at Burke's heart, but he forced himself to turn from her and tell the emergency medical technicians what he knew. The two EMTs rolled a stretcher close to the car and bent to retrieve John Hayes, but Missy screamed and refused to let go of her father.

Burke finally yanked her away and held her writhing, kicking body as the EMT's loaded her dad into the ambulance. The moment the ambulance pulled out of the parking lot, all the starch went out of the child. With nimble, monkey-like movements, she spun around in Burke's arms and latched onto his neck, wrapping both legs around his waist and sobbing against the collar of his coat.

"My daddy. They'll kill my daddy."

"Shh." Burke rubbed her back and did his best to comfort her. "Everything will be fine, Missy. Don't worry. Everything will be just fine."

He glanced up and watched a deputy sheriff pull into the parking lot. Relieved to see it was someone he knew, Burke continued patting the little girl's back as he stood outside the car that had been her home for far too long.

"Hey, Tip. What's going on?" Deputy Tim Turner asked as he approached them with a notepad and a smile.

The sound of another voice caused Missy to raise her head and give the deputy a watery perusal. She buried her head beneath Burke's chin, scowling at the other officer.

Burke glanced down at her then at the deputy. "Thanks for coming, Tim. I found a Caucasian male, approximately early thirties, unconscious, in the back of this vehicle. He and his daughter," he glanced down again, "have been living in this car for a while. Missy doesn't have any other family."

"I see," Tim said, taking down notes for a report. "And the ambulance took her father…"

"John Hayes," Burke supplied.

Tim nodded. "Her father is on his way to the hospital?"

At the mention of hospital, Missy broke into a fresh round of tears. Burke glared at the deputy and returned to offering comforting reassurances to the child.

"You know the routine, Tip," Tim said, waggling his pen in the direction of the sobbing child.

"I do know it, Tim." Burke tried to hold Missy away from him, but she clung to his neck with a strength that shocked him. "Deputy Turner is going to take you to a nice warm office and they'll find you a wonderful place to stay until your dad is well and can get you."

"No!" she protested. "You can't make me go. I'll stay in the car until Daddy is better. He'll know how to find me here. I won't go!"

Tim pocketed his notepad and reached out to take the child from Burke. As soon as his hands touched her, she screamed as though the grim reaper had laid his hands on her, drawing gazes from people all over the parking lot of the truck stop.

On the verge of hysteria, she clung so tightly to Burke, he could barely breathe let alone offer much help to the deputy. The two men tried to pry her loose, but she refused to be moved.

"Come on, now, Missy. Don't be so upset. You'll be taken care of and have a warm place to sleep and plenty to eat," the deputy said in a voice edged with annoyance. With each tug he made, Missy's screams increased in volume until both men cringed.

Finally, Burke shook his head and wrapped his arms comfortingly around the child. "Shh, Missy. Calm down. Just take a deep breath and calm down."

She stopped screaming, but sucked air in short, terrified gasps.

Burke looked to the deputy. "Tim, do you suppose, just this once, you might let me handle this and allow me to take her in tomorrow morning? Things have a way of seeming less traumatic early in the day."

"That they do," Tim said, nodding in agreement. "Are you planning to keep her this evening?"

"Maybe, but I have a friend who'd be better suited to taking care of her. If Ellen can come over, I'll handle the situation for now. Can you text me the address of where we'll need to go in the morning?"

"Yeah, I can do that." The deputy removed his hat and ran a hand over his head while studying Burke. "Are you sure, Tip? We can go for the ripping a Band-Aid method if you want." The deputy made a forceful tugging motion with his hand.

At Burke's shake of his head, Tim sighed. "I've never known you to get personally involved in a case before."

"I know, Tim, but I'll make an exception just this once if you will."

Tim nodded. "Fine by me. I'll swing by the hospital and find out how things are going there and let you know later."

"I'd really appreciate it, man. Thanks."

"Don't thank me. You're the one in for a long night." Tim moved closer to his car. "Are you on duty tomorrow?"

"No, it's my day off."

Tim grinned. "Good luck, then."

The deputy left and Burke continued holding Missy a few more minutes before he set her down.

Much to his relief, she turned loose of him and again used her mittens to mop the tears from her face.

Burke hunkered down so they were on eye level. "Just for tonight, Missy, you can stay at my place. I'll see if my friend will come and hang out with us. How does that sound?"

"Okay," she whispered, scuffing her toe in circles on the bleak pavement. "I just want my daddy back."

"I know, honey, but your dad is very sick and he needs to get well first." Burke straightened and pointed to the car. "Do you have a suitcase? We better pack up your stuff."

"In the trunk," Missy said, taking the keys from the ignition and scurrying around to the back of the car. She wiggled the key in the lock and turned it. Burke heard a raspy click then pushed up the lid of the trunk.

As he stared down at the few boxes of belongings that had once been part of a happy family, his heart constricted in pain. It must have been so hard for Missy's dad to condense his entire life into what would fit in the trunk of the junky old car.

Burke spied a flowered suitcase and lifted it out of the trunk. "Anything else you want to take with you?" he asked, looking at Missy.

The child climbed up on the bumper and reached into a box full of photographs, she snagged the top two, then hopped down and raced back around, climbing inside the car and stuffing things into a purple backpack. She snatched her fleece snowflake blanket off the seat then slid back out of the car. The backpack looked as though it might topple her backwards with the weight of it, but she leaned forward to maintain her balance.

Burke shut the trunk lid, made sure the car was locked, and lifted the suitcase in one hand along with her backpack. He reached out with the other and took Missy's hand. "Ready to go?"

"I guess so," she said, casting one last, longing glance at the car before following Burke to his pickup.

He set her suitcase and backpack in the backseat, tossed the blanket on top, then lifted Missy up to the front passenger seat. "Buckle in," he advised.

She rolled her eyes and snapped the buckle in place. "Duh! I'm not a baby, you know."

Rather than respond, Burke briefly wondered if he and his siblings had been as annoying to his parents when they were Missy's age. Ruefully, he concluded they were probably far more so.

"Where are we going?" Missy asked as Burke pulled out on the road and headed toward his house.

The little girl strained to see out the window. Burke should have looked to see if she had a booster seat in the old car, but hadn't even thought about it until now.

He pulled up at his house a short while later and parked, turning off the lights in the evening's inky darkness. "Here we are," he said, opening his door.

Missy opened her door and jumped down while Burke gathered her things. Together, they walked to the front door. Burke unlocked it, clicked on the light, and watched as Missy hesitantly stepped inside.

"This is your house?" she asked, walking around the living room, staring at the photos taken at the ranch hanging on the walls.

"'It is my house, at least for now."

Missy noticed his Stetson hanging on a hook by the door. She turned back to him with a grin. "Are you a real cowboy?"

"Yep. I sure am." He set down her things then pointed to a photo across the room that was taken of him on the back of a cutting horse as he helped work cattle. He'd been about fifteen at the time. "That's me right there."

"Wow," she said, awed as she studied the photograph. "You were cute, for a boy."

Burke grinned. "Thanks, I think. Does that mean I'm not cute anymore?"

Missy rolled her eyes and followed him down the hall to the kitchen. "No. It means you're a man. Men aren't cute, are they? Aren't you supposed to call them handsome?"

"I suppose so." He turned on the kitchen light then the light in the utility room. His hand hovered on the knob as he glanced down at Missy. "Are you scared of dogs?"

"No. I love animals. We had a kitty, but had to get rid of Whiskers when Mommy got sick." The lip began to edge out in a pout again, so Burke opened the door and whistled.

Lovey raced across the yard and leaped up the back step, sliding into the house and across the floor, landing in a wiggling heap at Missy's feet.

The child's face lit with a broad smile as she dropped to the floor and began petting the dog. Big green eyes glanced up at him, full of life and happiness. "She's so pretty. What's her name?"

"Lovey. She won't bite, but don't pull her ears or tail."

Missy gave him a look that let him know she thought he was dumber than a box full of rocks and continued petting the dog.

While Lovey entertained the little girl, Burke moved into the kitchen and called Ellen.

She answered on the third ring, sounding slightly out of breath. Under normal circumstances, that fact would have provided an interesting distraction and sent his blood zinging through his veins, but not tonight.

Tonight, he had a child in his care and no idea what to do with her.

Chapter Seven

Ellen shivered as she dripped water all over her floor. She'd just stepped out of the shower when she heard her phone ring. Afraid it might be Burke calling to cancel again, she snatched up a towel and raced to answer her phone.

He'd warned her he sometimes had to work late or got an unexpected call to work, so she'd be able to temper her disappointment if he couldn't make it. So far, he'd had to call at the last minute and cancel their last two dates. She knew he was disappointed, too, but it didn't make it any easier when all she wanted to do was spend time with him.

In fact, she hadn't seen him since the night, actually it was morning if one wanted to get technical, he'd walked her to her door and kissed her more passionately and thoroughly than she'd ever been kissed in her life.

Eager to experience more of those bone-melting kisses, she hoped he wasn't planning to cancel again.

"Hello?" Ellen answered, breathless from her sprint across her bedroom and down the hall to the entry where she'd left her phone on the little table by the door. She'd been in such a rush to get ready for her date, she'd forgotten to take the phone with her to the bedroom.

"Hey, Ellen, it's Burke. I'm not going to be able to make it for our date tonight." He paused and released a long breath. She could picture him running a hand over his short, dark hair. "Do you know anything about little girls?"

"As a matter of fact, I do know a thing or two about little girls. You won't believe it, but I used to be one."

"Very funny," Burke said, sounding less than humored.

"Why are you asking?" Ellen padded back to her bathroom and grabbed a towel, dabbing at her wet hair.

"Because I have one here with me and don't know, exactly, what to do with her."

Ellen frowned. "Are you at home?"

"Yeah. It's kind of a long story. Tomorrow, I'll take her to Child Protective Services and they'll place her in a foster home, but for tonight, she's staying with me."

"Would you like me to come over? Maybe I could help you keep her entertained."

A sigh of relief rolled out of Burke. "I'd love that, Ellen. I really am sorry about our date. I was looking forward to not watching the movie while trying to steal a kiss or two from you."

"Officer Burke! Are you thirteen or thirty?" she admonished.

"Neither. I'm twenty-eight and there's nothing wrong with wanting to kiss the prettiest girl who's ever tried to plow right over me and Bear."

Ellen laughed softly. "If you give me an hour, I'll pick up some dinner and bring it over."

"That would be great. Do you remember how to get here?"

"Vaguely," Ellen hung up the silk blouse she'd laid out to wear with a pair of black dress pants and pulled out a thick red sweater and a pair of jeans instead. "Would you mind texting me the address? My GPS should get me there with no problem. If I get lost, I'll call."

Burke's voice no longer rang with a hint of panic. "Perfect. I'll see you in a bit. And Ellen?"

"Yes?" she asked, plugging in her blow dryer.

"You're awesome. Thank you for being so understanding." His voice dropped to a husky tone that made goose bumps pop out all over her skin. "I'll try to find a way to make this up to you."

"You're welcome and I'll hold you to that."

She quickly phoned in an order for takeout Chinese food, blow-dried her hair then dressed. A quick swipe or two of mascara and a light spritz of perfume left her ready. She shoved her arms into her coat sleeves, wrapped a scarf around her neck, and ran out the door.

Thirty minutes later, she pulled up outside Burke's house. She'd barely opened her car door when he jogged outside. She handed him one of the bags of food and accepted the kiss he pressed to her cheek with a sense of pleasure.

"You're just glad to see me because I came bearing food," she teased as they hurried down the walk.

"That's not true at all. I'm excited to see you because Missy has threatened to make me play Barbies with her and, having grown up with a little sister, I know exactly what that misery entails."

Ellen laughed. "You really are in dire straits, then, aren't you?"

"You have no idea," he said, leaning so close, his lips brushed her ear. "I really was looking forward to a date with you Ellen. You look incredible."

She blushed and stepped inside where an adorable little girl with dark blonde hair and green eyes that put her in mind of Christmas holly stood with one small hand burrowed into Lovey's thick fur.

"Hi, I'm Ellen, Officer Tipton's friend." Ellen smiled brightly, hoping to put the child at ease.

"You're pretty," the girl said, then glanced over at Burke. "You have better taste than I thought."

Ellen's eyes widened in surprise and, for a moment, Burke looked as though he'd swallowed something entirely distasteful before he schooled his features to a neutral expression.

The child smiled and stretched out her hand toward Ellen. "I'm Missy."

"It's nice to meet you, Missy. Do you like Chinese food?" Ellen asked, taking the small hand in hers then leading the way to the kitchen.

"I love Chinese food! We haven't had it since before Mommy went away." The child stayed close to Ellen as she set out the food while Burke got out plates and cutlery.

"Do you like milk, Missy?" he asked, opening the refrigerator door.

"Yes, please," she said, taking a seat at the small table in Burke's kitchen. Lovey strolled beneath it and lay down with a contented sigh. Burke filled two glasses with milk then held one out to Ellen. She nodded and he poured a third, setting them on the table.

"This smells so good, Ellen. Thank you for bringing it," he said, disappearing and returning with a stack of books. "Here, Missy, try sitting on these so you can reach the table better."

"Thanks," the little girl said, hopping off the chair. Burke placed the books then lifted her to sit on top of them. "That's better!"

Burke seated Ellen then they passed around the food. Ellen watched the child ravenously eat her food. Fearful she'd make herself sick, Ellen leaned toward her. "Missy, I think you have the loveliest green eyes I've ever seen."

The child stuffed another forkful of food in her mouth, giving her a suspicious glance.

"You don't believe me?" Ellen asked.

Missy shook her head and took another bite.

"Well, I don't lie. I'll even prove it to you." Ellen pulled her phone from her pocket and scrolled through images until she found one of her and Tara together. She handed the phone to the child. "That's my best friend, Tara. She has beautiful green eyes, don't you think?"

Missy stared at the image then nodded slowly. Before she could hand the phone back to Ellen, Burke took it, curious to see the woman Ellen spoke of so frequently. The two girls looked so different. Ellen was petite, elegant, and sophisticated. Tara was tall, graceful, and lively.

Burke handed the phone to Ellen and she left it on the table by her plate, turning her attention back to the child "Tara's pretty, isn't she?"

"She's beautiful," Missy said, taking a bite of her third egg roll.

"Tara definitely is, but I think your eyes are even prettier than hers." Ellen winked at Missy. "Just don't tell her I said that. I wouldn't want to hurt her feelings."

"I won't tell," Missy said, ducking her head to hide her smile.

"So, Missy, is that your full name?" Ellen asked, casually prying for more information. Burke would fill her in later on what he knew, but she had an idea she might get more detail out of the child than he could.

"No. I'm Missy Hayes." The little girl gave her a rueful glare. "Everyone has a last name, unless you're famous. Then you only have to use one name."

"True," Ellen agreed. "Will I someday be standing in line at the grocery store, pick up a magazine, and see a headline about Missy?"

The little girl laughed. "No, don't be silly. I'd have to change my name to something special."

"I think your name is special," Burke said, joining the conversation.

Missy rolled her eyes at him then turned back to Ellen. "What's your name?"

"Ellen Juliet Meade."

"That's a good name," Missy said, studying Ellen. "You look like an Ellen. You have pretty eyes, too."

"That's what I told her," Burke muttered, earning a frown from Missy and a smile from Ellen.

Ellen directed the conversation back to the child. "Does Missy stand for something, like Melissa?"

Missy wrinkled up her nose. "Not Melissa. There's a Melissa in my class at school. She thinks she's queen of everything and is always bossing everyone around. She told me I had to sit at the back of the classroom because she didn't want to have to see my hair."

"Did you move to the back of the classroom?" Ellen asked, knowing she would have at Missy's age.

"Of course not," Missy said, leaning back in her chair. She swung her little fist in the air. "I popped her in the nose and told her I'd sit wherever I want to."

Burke swallowed down the words of praise that sprang to his lips, especially at Ellen's warning glower.

Ellen placed a hand over Missy's as it rested on the table. "Did she leave you alone after that?"

"Yep. Everyone sits where they want because she's afraid to be bossy, at least when I'm around." Missy toyed with her fork and glanced at Ellen. "My name isn't really Missy."

Burke sat a little straighter at this news. Perhaps the child had been kidnapped. Maybe she'd been coached on what to say in case she was separated from her captor. "What do you mean? What's your name?"

"Mistletoe," the child whispered, glancing down at her plate. "My real name is Mistletoe."

Burke slumped in relief while Ellen smiled. She lifted the child's chin with her finger until green eyes met brown. "I love that name, Missy. Why did your parents name you Mistletoe?"

In light of the two adults smiling at her instead of making fun of her name, she relaxed. "I was born on Christmas Day. Mommy told Daddy he could choose my name. He laughed and said I was his little bundle of Mistletoe. Mistletoe Marie Hayes." The child poked a finger into her chest. "That's me. But everyone calls me Missy."

"It's a wonderful name, Missy, especially this time of year," Ellen assured the child. "It's much more fun than having a plain old name like Ellen."

"Oh, but Ellen is such a nice name. It sounds like a name a mom might have." Missy studied Ellen for a few quiet moments. "Do you know how to bake cookies?"

Ellen laughed. "I certainly do. My friend, Tara, the one with the green eyes, is a pastry chef. And she worked in a bakery for a while. She taught me how to bake a few things."

"That's so cool," Missy said then looked at Burke. "Isn't it?"

"It is."Burke tossed a teasing wink at Ellen that made her inside flutter in delight. "Anytime you want to show off your mad cookie-baking skills, I'm happy to do some taste-testing."

"Good to know," Ellen said, taking a bite of egg foo yung.

Later, after she'd helped Missy take a bath and get ready for bed, she and Burke listened to the child say her bedtime prayers. Her little voice broke as she asked God to watch over her daddy and keep him safe. Ellen forced her gaze up to the ceiling in an effort to keep her tears at bay. Her heart ached for the little girl.

While she'd splashed in a tub full of bubbles, thanks to a bottle of bubble bath Bella had left behind, Missy had told Ellen about her mother dying, living in the old car, and her father getting sick. Ellen hastened to reiterate what Burke had said, that the doctors would help her father and everything would be fine.

Once Missy finished with her prayers, she climbed into the bed and sighed contentedly as she settled against the fluffy pillows and soft sheets. Burke pulled up the comforter while Ellen tucked it around her.

"How's that?" Ellen asked, taking a seat on the edge of the bed.

"Nice," Missy murmured sleepily.

Ellen brushed her fingers along the child's brow, fanning little wisps that had escaped the braid she'd woven in Missy's long hair after they'd washed it and toweled it dry.

"Tell me a story, please?" Missy asked on a whisper.

Ellen looked to Burke and he shrugged, at a loss for what to do. Suddenly, he grinned and raced out of the room. Missy sat up and watched the door, listening with Ellen at the sound of the back door banging. In a matter of minutes, Burke returned carrying a large plastic tote.

"I should have remembered this sooner," he said, setting the storage box on the floor by the bed and lifting the lid. He dug through toys and finally unearthed a handful of storybooks. He sorted through them then held one out to Missy.

"How about this one?" he asked.

She studied the cover then grinned at him and nodded. "But only if you read it."

"Okay," he said, taking a seat on the bed on the other side of her.

Ellen tucked her back in and sat with an arm around Missy's small shoulders while Burke leaned against the headboard and read a book about a horse who accompanied the three wise men on their journey.

When he finished, Missy released a sweet sigh and nestled down into her covers.

Ellen bent over and kissed her forehead, brushing the hair from her face one more time before she rose from the bed.

Burke kissed the child's rosy cheek and carefully stood. They moved the storage tote over to the closet and edged toward the door.

"I think she's asleep," Ellen whispered, quietly backing out of the guest room beside Burke.

He pulled the door shut, leaving it open just enough a trickle of light from the hall spilled into the room, keeping it from being shrouded in darkness.

Neither of them spoke as they made their way to the kitchen where Ellen helped Burke clean up the dinner dishes.

It wasn't until they were seated on the couch, Burke with a bottle of Dr. Pepper and Ellen with a cup of spicy tea, that they discussed Missy. Burke relayed what little he knew. The deputy had phoned to let him know the father had pneumonia.

"Tim said the doctor thinks it will be a week, maybe more, before they can release him. In the meantime, Missy will have to go into the foster system." Burke took a sip of his pop.

Ellen frowned. "I hate to see that happen. She doesn't have any relatives who can take her in?"

"Evidently not. Tim couldn't turn up anyone living, anyway. He verified what Missy told us. The kid didn't lie about any of it. Her father was a manager at a pretend sporting goods store before he quit to take care of his wife."

Ellen gave him a quizzical look. "A pretend sporting goods store? What on earth is that?"

Burke grinned. "You know, those stores that pretend to be a sporting goods store but only sell trendy workout clothes and wimpy gym equipment as well as stuff for kids' sports. Where I grew up, when you said you were going to a sporting goods store, it meant there would be an entire fishing and camping section, a gun library, and taxidermy animals galore."

"That's disgusting," Ellen said, grimacing. She took a sip of tea and redirected the conversation. "What will happen to Missy until her dad is back on his feet?"

"Like I said, she'll enter the foster system. I sure hate to see it happen this close to Christmas, but there isn't much else that can be done."

Ellen leaned back, thinking of all the things that could go wrong for both Missy and her father. "Will you keep an eye on her, Burke? I don't want her to get lost in the system."

"I don't either." Burke took her hand in his and raised it to his lips. "I'll do my best to keep track of her. Maybe, if you're game for it, we could visit her or take her out to do something. I just hate for the poor kid to feel abandoned."

Ellen leaned her head on his shoulder. "I'd love to go with you. Perhaps we could take her on some sort of fun Christmas outing."

"She'd probably love it. Understandably, the kid really seems to be into Christmas." Burke shifted his arm so it wrapped around Ellen's shoulders, pulling her closer.

"This is nice," she whispered, listening to the strong, steady beat of his heart beneath her ear as her head rested on his muscled chest. She breathed in his enticing, rugged scent and closed her eyes, imagining how it would feel to fall asleep every night in his arms.

Hours later, Ellen awoke with a start. Her eyes flew open and she looked around in panic until she recalled she was at Burke's place.

Beside her, he breathed softly, evenly, his head tilted at an odd angle against the back of the couch. They'd both need to visit a massage therapist after cricking their necks all night. Lest she disturb him, Ellen slowly raised up, discovering they'd been covered with a fleece blanket printed with white snowflakes on a blue background. A lamp glowed across the room, although someone had turned off the overhead light.

Since Ellen had been drooling, both literally and figuratively, over Burke, she had to assume Missy had been the one who covered them up and turned off the lights.

Ellen stood and silently made her way to the bathroom. When she opened the door, she found Lovey waiting for her.

"Poor girl. Did we forget about you?" she asked in a whisper as she rubbed the dog's head then let her escape out the back door to do her business.

In the kitchen, she checked the time on the stove, shocked as the clock confirmed it was almost six in the morning.

She'd been on two dates with Burke, if last night's babysitting could be considering a date, and both times he'd kept her out all night.

Too bad this time she wouldn't even get a sizzling goodbye kiss.

Uncertain if she should leave while he and Missy both slept or stay, Missy made the decision for her when she rushed out of the guest room, sobbing.

Ellen hurried down the hall and dropped to her knees as Missy ran to her, burying her face against Ellen's shoulder.

"Shh, sweetheart. Shh. It's okay. Everything is going to be okay. I promise." Ellen pulled the child onto her lap and rocked her. She held her close and stroked her disheveled hair.

Burke suddenly appeared and dropped to one knee, placing a hand on Missy's back while his eyes collided with Ellen's. His still bore a fog of sleep, but the warmth in them was undeniable.

"What's all this about, Mistletoe?" he asked in a voice husky with sleep and fatigue.

"I had a bad dream," the child said, sniffling as she curtailed her tears. "I have them sometimes."

"It's okay, Missy. I have bad dreams too, sometimes," Ellen said, using the palms of her hands to brush away the little girl's tears. She wrapped the child in a warm hug, kissed the top of her head, then glanced at Burke.

The way he studied her made heat start to bubble in her belly and slowly spread to every extremity. Unsettled by it, Ellen set Missy on her feet and stood.

"Since we're all awake, why don't we make some breakfast? That's if Officer Tipton has something besides cold cereal to eat."

"I'll have you know I've got plenty of eggs, bacon, ham, and bread." Burke rose and lifted Missy in his arms, tickling her sides to chase away the remnants of fright and sadness brought on by her dream.

Together, the three of them made scrambled eggs, crispy bacon, and French toast. Burke was on his third helping of French toast when Missy looked at Ellen and giggled.

"What's so funny?" he asked, drizzling syrup over the bread, then glancing from Ellen to Missy.

Missy shrugged and broke off a piece of bacon, giggling again as she shoved it in her mouth.

Burke turned a questioning gaze to Ellen, but she focused on the sugar she stirred into a cup of tea.

"Mmm. This tea really is delicious. It tastes like Christmas."

Missy lifted her head, trying to stare in Ellen's cup. "How can tea taste like Christmas?"

"It just does." Ellen took another sip, then got up and poured a little bit of her tea into a cup and handed it to the child. "Try it."

Missy's eyes lit with pleasure as she tried the tea. "It does taste like Christmas. Like gingerbread cookies and cinnamon bread, and Santa's secret ingredients."

"That's exactly what I think," Ellen said, smiling at Missy as she trailed a hand over the child's head.

After breakfast, Missy got dressed while Burke and Ellen washed the dishes. The child bundled up then went outside to play with Lovey. Burke and Ellen stood close together, watching the dog and child play together.

"When do you need to take her in?" Ellen asked, hating that one of them couldn't keep Missy until her dad was well. Between her job and Burke's, though, there was no possibility of making that work.

"I told the deputy I'd have her there before ten this morning. Waiting until the last second to leave her there won't make it any easier."

"No, it won't," Ellen agreed. "But you'll make sure you know where she's at and that we can visit her sometimes?"

"I promise I will," Burke said, putting his arm around Ellen and pulling her against him. She wrapped her arms around his lean waist and soaked up his strength.

Even though she'd only met Missy last night, already the child had firmly planted herself in Ellen's tender heart. If she wasn't mistaken, the same thing had happened to Burke.

"Are you working next weekend?" she asked, abruptly changing the subject.

"On Saturday, but I have Sunday through Tuesday off. Why?" Burke lowered his head until his chin rested on top of her fragrant hair.

"I thought we could take Missy to do something. Like pick out a Christmas tree or go for a walk in the park. She'd probably be thrilled if you brought Lovey along."

Burke kissed the top of Ellen's head. "Let's plan on something Sunday afternoon. Why don't I pick you up at your place, we can take Missy out, then the two of us can have dinner together."

"That sounds perfect." Ellen pulled back from him. "I really should get going. For the record, I'd like to state I never stay out all night on a first date, or second date, or any date, for that matter."

Burke laughed. "Yeah? Being with you just makes the time fly by." He kissed her cheek. "I'll go get your coat if you want to tell Missy you're leaving."

Ellen gathered her things and left her purse by the door, then slipped on the coat Burke held for her.

He waited inside as Ellen opened the back door and stepped out. Lovey and Missy ran over to her, both excited.

"Come play with us, Ellen. Please?" Missy asked, tugging on Ellen's hand.

"Oh, Missy, I wish I could, but I have to go home."

The child's big green eyes filled with tears and her bottom lip slid into a pout. "Can't you stay? Just a little longer?"

"I really do have to go, Missy, but I promise you'll see me again. Now that we've met, you won't be able to get rid of me." Ellen bent down and pulled the child to her, enfolding her in a loving embrace.

"You promise?" Missy asked in a small, scared voice.

"I promise, Missy. Cross my heart and everything," Ellen said, cupping the little girl's chin and raising it upward. She kissed her cold button nose then straightened, holding out a hand to her.

"Want to walk me to my car?"

Missy gave her another hug then stepped back with a grin. "Nope. Tip can't give you a kiss if I'm around. I can tell he really likes you. When he thinks you aren't watching, he looks at you like this."

The little girl pulled a comical cross-eyed kissy face that made Ellen burst into laughter.

"If you say so," she said, hugging the child one more time. She took a business card from her pocket and handed it to Missy. "If you need anything at all, you call me anytime. My cell phone is the number on the bottom."

"Thanks, Ellen." Missy tucked the card in her coat pocket and returned to playing with the dog.

Ellen went inside and found Burke watching through the kitchen window.

He turned to her with a baffled expression. "Isn't she going to walk out with us?"

"She assured me you should show me out by yourself." Ellen moved down the hall to the living room, gathered her purse and scarf, then opened the front door.

"What, exactly, does Missy think we're going to do if I walk you to the car without her and Lovey serving as chaperones?" Burke asked.

"She mentioned something about a kiss." Ellen's cheeks turned pink at the admission as she unlocked her car and started it so it could warm up. The December air was chilly and the wind held a cold bite to it as she got back out and faced Burke. "I think you've got a future hopeless romantic on your hands."

"Heaven help us all if that's true." Burke rolled his eyes with a dramatic groan for emphasis.

Ellen laughed and shrugged deeper into the warmth of her coat.

Burke pulled her into his arms and held her close a minute. She relished the contact, the opportunity to fill her nose and memory with his scent before she left. They remained that way for a long moment before Ellen stepped back.

"Promise you'll call me as soon as you know anything about Missy's situation and how her father is doing."

"I promise, Ellen." He gently brushed his thumb across her cheek as sparks of interest and longing began to burn in his eyes. "You better get going. It's too cold to stand around out here and besides, I have a feeling we're being closely watched."

They both turned and caught Missy standing on something, peering over the backyard fence.

Ellen waved at her, pecked Burke on the cheek, and then got into her car.

Dating Burke was proving to be far more interesting than she'd ever imagined.

Chapter Eight

The day Burke left Missy at Child Protective Services, she'd clung to him, begging him to take her until her father was well.

Tempted to give in to her pleas, common sense prevailed. He had no one to watch her from the time she got out of school until he got off work. Even if he did, he had no idea about caring for a child. Ellen had done most of the nurturing and guiding the one night Missy spent at his house. Then again, the child seemed more like she was six going on thirty a lot of the time.

With his heart breaking at the sound of her cries, he left her with a caseworker and a promise he'd check on her soon.

Although he didn't go to the foster home where she was staying, he did touch base nearly every day with the caseworker, who assured him Missy was doing as well as was expected under the circumstances.

Burke also went to the hospital to visit her father. The man was making progress and would soon be well enough to release, but he was nearly frantic about Missy. Burke did his best to reassure John that

Missy was being taken care of and vowed to keep an eye on her.

Sunday, he went to friend's ranch south of the city, looking for a little help to pull off a surprise for Ellen and Missy. He'd arranged for Missy to spend the afternoon with him and Ellen. They'd feed her lunch, have a fun adventure, then take her back to the foster home in time for dinner. Since he didn't know if he'd have another opportunity to spend time with her, pending her father's release from the hospital, Burke wanted to make the most of it.

What he had planned would most likely also make Ellen smile. She'd told him how much she'd loved riding horses at summer camp. He just hoped her skills weren't too rusty for what he wanted to do.

Ellen would pick up Missy right after church and bring her over to Burke's place. He sent Ellen a quick text that morning telling her to dress in jeans and sturdy shoes and to make sure she had a warm coat and gloves.

He'd just returned from Cooper's place and parked on the street in front of his house when Ellen pulled into his driveway. She'd barely turned off the ignition when Missy barreled out of the car and raced over to him. Burke swung her up into a tight hug and kissed her cheek.

"Well, Miss Mistletoe, how are you?" he asked, carrying her back to where Ellen removed a duffle bag from the backseat of her car.

"I'm great! At least now that I get to spend the day with both of you," Missy said, giving him another hug. Her eyes swung over to the horse trailer behind his pickup where the sounds of horses moving reached her ears. "Are there really horses in there?"

"You bet there are." He grinned at her as he held out a hand to Ellen. "Would you like to meet my partner, Sugar Bear, and his friend, Comet?"

Missy nodded her head up and down, bouncing in Burke's arms. He walked over to the horse trailer and lifted her up so she could look inside.

"Oh, they're beautiful," she whispered. She glanced down at Burke. "What are you going to do with them?"

"We're going to have lunch, then go for a ride."

"Really?" Missy spun around in Burke's arms and gave him a hug.

Much to his delight, Ellen appeared as though she'd like to do the same. He made note of the fact she still wore a dress and heels with a long wool coat.

"Come on, ladies, let's go inside and eat, then we can head out to play."

"Sounds perfect, Burke," Ellen said, smiling at him with such warmth, he wondered if his heart might melt into a syrupy pool.

On his way back home with the horses, he'd stopped and purchased what he considered picnic fare, thinking it might be fun to have an indoor picnic. He spread a blanket on the floor in the living room and set out the food while Ellen changed out of the dress that accentuated her beauty, making him painfully aware of how much he'd like to hold and kiss her.

But today wasn't about their budding relationship. It was about Missy.

Ellen returned with her hair in a long braid down her back. She wore jeans, a chunky sweater almost the same shade of green as Missy's eyes, and a pair of cowboy boots that looked as though they'd had a considerable amount of wear. Burke gawked at her choice of footwear, but managed to snap his mouth shut and hand her a plate as she sank down on the other side of Missy.

The three of them enjoyed fried chicken, corn, potatoes, and biscuits. After the dishes were washed and the leftover food put away, Ellen made sure Missy was sufficiently bundled against the cold. She borrowed a scarf of Burke's to wrap around the child's neck before they went outside.

"Almost forgot someone," Burke said, opening a side gate on the yard and whistling.

Lovey raced out and yipped with glee when she spied Ellen and Missy. Missy dropped down and hugged the dog, scrunching her nose as Lovey washed her face with slobbery kisses.

"Load up, Lovey," Burke said and tapped the side of the pickup. The dog took a few running steps and leaped into the back, happily running from one side to the other. "On second thought, it's probably safer if you ride inside, Lovey."

Burke opened the back passenger door and the dog sailed out of the pickup then jumped into the back, settling on an old blanket Burke tossed onto the seat.

Ellen helped Missy into the back then took Burke's hand as he helped her into the front passenger seat.

"Are we ready for an adventure?" he asked.

Missy cheered and clapped her hands while Ellen tossed him a coy smile. "I've yet to be around you and not have one."

"Just part of my irresistible charm, Ellen."

An hour and a half later, Ellen and Missy gaped in surprise as Burke parked the pickup.

"Well, what do you think?" he asked as he unfastened his seatbelt.

"I think you're a genius," Ellen said, pecking his cheek while excitement glistened in her eyes. "Snow. I can't believe you brought us up here in the snow."

"It wouldn't be a Christmassy kind of horseback ride if we didn't have snow. Mount Hood has some great trails. When I heard there was a fall of new snow, I decided I had to bring you girls up here."

"Do we really get to ride the horses in the snow?" Missy asked, leaning over the seat between the two of them.

Burke tweaked her nose. "We sure do. Pull on your mittens and wrap that scarf around your neck. It'll be cold out there."

"Okay!" Missy said, quickly following his instructions while Ellen did the same.

Burke opened Ellen's door and helped her out then swung Missy to the ground before he went back to get the horses. Lovey jumped down and raced around in the snow, barking and yipping.

Missy giggled when the dog dipped her face in the snow then came up wearing a white beard and mustache. "Lovey, you're silly," the little girl chided, brushing the snow off the dog.

"Don't get wet, Missy. We don't want you to get cold on the ride. If you aren't frozen when we finish, you can play in the snow then." Burke cautioned the child as he led out first Sugar Bear and then Comet. Ellen closed the horse trailer gate then stood back, admiring both horses.

"Where did you get this horse? Is he a member of the Mounted Patrol Unit, too?" she asked, holding out a hand for the horse to sniff then gently scratching the neck of the beautiful sorrel paint gelding.

"No. Comet belongs to a friend. Cooper lives down near St. Paul. He and his grandfather have a ranch. This time of year, he's in Las Vegas for the rodeo, but he sent me a text that it was okay to borrow Comet today."

"What does Cooper do?" Ellen asked as Missy started to race over to the horses.

Burke caught her with one arm then set her down, keeping a hold on her shoulder. "Missy, horses can get spooked real easy, so you can't scream or squeal or race right up to them. They like you to approach slow and easy. Okay?

"Okay," the little girl said, walking with exaggeratedly slow steps over to Ellen.

With a smile, she lifted the little girl so she could pet Comet.

"He's a clown," Burke said, drawing Ellen's attention back to him.

"The horse?" she asked, confused.

Burke chuckled. "No, Cooper. He's a rodeo clown, although the correct term is barrelman. He's a really good one, too."

"Oh, wow. That seems like a dangerous profession," she said, then realized it probably didn't seem any more dangerous than a police officer or fireman for that matter.

"It can be, but Cooper really is good at what he does." Burke yanked on a pair of gloves and snapped up his coat then tugged down his Stetson. "Are you two girls ready to ride?"

"More than ready," Ellen said, wishing she'd worn an extra pair of socks, but not willing to miss the chance to ride for anything.

Burke helped her up on Sugar Bear then handed her the reins. "He's easy to ride and hard to spook. I think you'll do fine on him. Need any instruction?"

Ellen adjusted her seat on the saddle and relaxed. "I'm hoping, like riding a bicycle, it will all come back to me."

Burke gave her a few quick pointers then scooped Missy up. He settled her on the back of Comet then swung up behind her. "You doing okay, Missy?"

"Oh, yes," the little girl said, so full of anticipation, she could hardly sit still.

"Then let's go explore," Burke said, clucking his tongue as Comet moved forward.

For the next hour, Burke led them on easy trails through the snow. They stopped to watch a deer and Ellen pointed out a pair of birds on a tree branch. The day couldn't have been more beautiful if Burke had special ordered it. The sun shone overhead, the breeze was nonexistent, and the temperature hovered just above the freezing point, meaning it wasn't horribly cold for either of the girls.

Ellen rode like she was born to it, with an easy hand on the reins, and a posture that would have put a ballerina to shame. Missy didn't say much, but each time Burke glanced down to check on her, the child's green eyes sparkled with enthusiasm and wonder.

"You warm enough, Missy?" he asked, and she bobbed her head, as though she was afraid of missing a single second of their ride.

When he rode back to the parking area, both Ellen and Missy looked disappointed. Yet, the rosy cheeks and red noses they sported confirmed his notion it was time to get them in out of the cold.

"This was the best day ever!" Missy proclaimed as Burke swung out of the saddle then lifted her to the ground. Lovey, who'd trailed along after them, ran circles around the child, trying to get her to play. While the two engaged in a snowy game of tag, Burke moved over to where Ellen reined in Sugar Bear and gave her a hand as she dismounted.

"I agree with Missy. It was the best day ever." Ellen leaned against him for just a moment.

"Legs feel a little weird?" he asked as Ellen struggled to take a step.

She grinned up at him. "Yes, they do. It's been too many years since I last rode, but the soreness tomorrow will be well worth it."

He bent down close to her ear. "If you need someone to help massage the sore muscles, I'm happy to volunteer."

She blushed and half-heartedly smacked his arm as he removed the saddle and bridle from Comet then did the same for Sugar Bear.

"Want to see something fun?" he asked.

"Of course," Ellen said while Missy bobbed her head up and down in agreement.

He led Sugar Bear over to a section of fence on the edge of the parking lot then whistled to Lovey. "Up you go, girl!"

The dog barked and ran to the horse. She sprang up on the fence, then placed her front paws on Sugar Bear's neck.

Missy and Ellen both clapped, then Missy cheered. "Do more, do more!"

"Get on up, Lovey," Burke encouraged the dog.

Lovey jumped onto the back of Sugar Bear then flopped down on his back, ears alert, tongue lolling out, proud of her accomplishments.

"Oh, that is fantastic," Ellen said, taking her phone from her pocket and snapping a few photos. "Did it take long to train them both to do that?"

"Not as long as you might think," Burke said, whistling once. Lovey jumped down to the ground and ran back over to Missy. "Bear enjoys it almost as much as Lovey."

"That was awesome!" Missy said, dropping to her knees and wrapping her arms around the dog.

Burke quickly loaded the horses then flipped up the console on the front seat and set Missy inside. He helped Ellen climb in before he slid behind the wheel and gave Missy an authoritative frown. "I want you to get as much heat as you can on your cold fingers and toes, Missy. However, under normal circumstances, you should ride in the backseat in a booster seat. Got it?"

"Yes, sir!" Missy said, and gave him a half-impressive salute.

Ellen turned to stare out the window to hide her laugh. When she glanced back and caught Burke's wink at her, she almost lost her ability to hold it in.

"Would anyone be up for some hot chocolate?" Burke asked as he pulled onto the road.

"Me! I would be!" Missy said, waving her hands above her head.

"With extra marshmallows?" Burke asked.

"Of course!" Missy proclaimed.

Later, after they'd enjoyed cups of hot chocolate and slices of pie at a restaurant on their way back to town, Ellen went with Burke to take Missy home. The goodbye was tearful, but Burke and Ellen both promised to visit her again.

Burke asked Ellen if she wanted to go with him to return the horses and she readily agreed. They stopped by the MPU barn and left Sugar Bear in his warm stall. The horse shook his mane and pranced around, as though he wanted to show off just for Ellen.

Strangely, Burke knew exactly how the horse felt.

Ellen looked with interest at the facility and Burke pointed out the highlights, introduced her to a few people, and then led her back out to the pickup where Cooper's horse and Lovey waited.

They drove to St. Paul and returned Comet to the ranch, spent a few moments speaking with Cooper's grandfather, then drove back to the MPU barn where Burke left the trailer.

"Want to join me for dinner?" Burke asked as they entered the freeway, heading back toward his place.

"I'd love to. I hate to leave Lovey in the pickup, though." Ellen reached back and scratched the dog's ears.

Burke grinned at the dog then let his gaze rest on her. Tendrils of hair escaped the confines of the braid she'd fashioned, dancing tantalizingly around her face. Cheeks remained pink from her afternoon outing, only enhancing the fine bone structure and incredible beauty of her face. Rich whiskey-hued eyes glowed with fun and life, and something Burke only dared dream was just for him. He wanted nothing more than to spend time with the enchanting woman.

"I don't want to leave Lovey in the pickup, either. I was thinking along the lines of something we could take to my place. In fact, if you aren't in a rush, we could get a few groceries and I'll cook dinner."

Ellen's eyebrows shot upwards. "You cook?"

"Sometimes, when the occasion calls for it."

Her playful grin made his heart skip a beat. "Then I hope this is the occasion."

After purchasing what he needed to create one of the few meals he could successfully make, Burke drove back to his place. Lovey kept step with Ellen as they walked inside the house, then the dog barked and raced to the utility room where she dug into her bowl of food.

Working together, Ellen and Burke prepared a dinner of steak and baked potatoes with buttery slices of French bread and, at her insistence he needed to eat more vegetables, green beans.

"This steak is so good, Burke. You can grill meat for me anytime," Ellen said, taking another bite of the juicy, tender steak.

"I'm happy to, anytime."

Once they finished their meal, Ellen helped Burke with the dishes. He made her a cup of tea and snagged a bottle of Dr. Pepper then they wandered into the living room. Lovey followed them, flopping down on her dog bed with an exhausted sigh.

"Today was wonderful, Burke. I'm not sure if Missy or I was the most excited."

"Definitely you," he teased.

She whopped him with a throw pillow and he grunted in feigned pain. "I've been assaulted by an elf."

"Who are you calling an elf, cowboy?" she asked, inflecting an extra portion of bravado into her voice.

"You, Elf," Burke taunted. "You looked rather elf-like today with those rosy cheeks and sparkling eyes." He leaned closer to her, brushing a wayward lock of hair behind her ear. "In fact, you looked so beautiful, you almost took my breath away."

"Burke," she whispered, her eyes shimmering with emotion. "That might be the nicest thing anyone has ever said to me."

"It's true, my little Christmas elf." His finger traced the outline of her ear. "If you added some pointy ears and shoes with bells on them, you'd be set. Why, I bet you could easily get a job helping Santa at the mall."

Ellen rolled her eyes and took a sip of her tea. "If I have to play an elf, then you have to play something, too." She studied him, tilting her head to one side. "You're too big to play an elf, and you'd make a horrible Santa."

Burke frowned. "Why couldn't I play Santa? I've got the laugh down. Just listen," he said. "Ho! Ho! Ho!" He blended just the right amount of belly deep humor with holiday fun in his impersonation.

She shrugged. "The laugh is good, nice and jolly, but you will never, ever pass as Santa looking like that."

"Like what?" he asked, glancing down and brushing a hand over his flat stomach.

"A handsome, fit, muscular, amazingly wonderful guy," she said, softly reaching out to clasp his hand. "What you did for Missy today was unforgettable, Burke. She'll treasure the memory for a lifetime."

"It wasn't much. The poor kid needed to get out and have some fun. I know her foster family is nice enough, but they are overcrowded and unable to give her much attention, especially with it being the holiday season." He cast a worried glance her way. "I'm concerned she's going to be there, or somewhere like it, much longer than anyone anticipated."

Ellen set her mug of tea on the table and gave Burke a questioning look. "What do you mean?"

He sighed and took a swig of his pop before setting the empty bottle on the coffee table. "I spoke with her father and the caseworker this morning. It seems Child Protective Services will not place Missy back with her father until he meets certain requirements."

"Such as?" Ellen asked.

"He has to be able to provide consistent food, clothing, and shelter for Missy. They want him to have a place to live, a steady income, and show that he can care for his daughter adequately." Burke sighed and leaned his head against the back of the couch. "It's going to be rough on both Missy and her father when they realize they can't immediately be back together. I understand why CPS makes rules like that, but Missy should be with her dad."

"Agreed. Does Mr. Hayes have an attorney?" Ellen asked, shifting from a woman enthralled with the handsome man beside her to attorney willing to fight tooth and nail for a client.

"No, he doesn't, but I have the name of an excellent attorney I'd be happy to recommend. With a little coercion, I'm hoping she'll even take on this case for free." Burke reached out and slid his hands around Ellen, drawing her closer to him.

The indulgent smile on her face coupled with her alluring scent all but obliterated his sense along with his restraint.

"How would you coerce her into volunteering for the job?" Ellen asked with mock innocence.

"Oh, I don't know. I suppose I could ply her with chocolates or dazzle her with flowers. She might be cooperative if I promised another day of horseback riding, or offered to grill steak for her again." He lifted her up and settled her across his lap, tipping her back so he could look into her face and fall into those magnificent eyes. "But I think this might work."

His head lowered toward hers and Ellen's eyes drifted shut as her arms slid around his neck. Rather than kiss her, as she expected, Burke buried his face against her neck and started tickling her sides.

She jumped then wriggled, trying to get away from him as she squealed and laughed.

"No, that definitely isn't it, Burke. Stop, stop, stop!"

When they both were breathless from laughing, he shifted her on his lap, maneuvering until their faces were just inches apart.

"Tickling is out. What do you think would work?" he asked in a ragged whisper, eyes focused on the pink perfection of her lips.

"This," she said, bracketing his face and rising up until her mouth brushed his. All pretense, all games, all silliness drifted away, replaced by a soul-deep yearning for each other. Sparks ignited as Burke took control of the kiss, wrapping her in his arms and lavishing her with his love.

Finally, Ellen pushed against his chest with a reluctant sigh. "As much as I hate to say it, Burke, I think it's best I head home."

"I don't want you to go," he rasped, eyes still glazed with the passion of their heated kisses.

"I don't want to go, but it's best that I do and we both know it. If you text me the info on Missy's dad, I'll see what I can do to help him." She stood and carried her now-cold cup of tea to the kitchen.

"I'll send you all the details this evening. He's due to be released from the hospital on Tuesday. If he and Missy want to spend Christmas together, he's going to have to find a job, a house, and show he's capable of properly caring for his daughter in just two weeks."

Ellen tossed him an impish grin. "Then as one of Santa's elves," she waved her hand at him, "and helper, we'd better get busy."

They returned to the living room and he held her coat while she slipped it on.

She gave him a long hug then stepped back. "Thank you, Burke, for a day I'll never forget and for making that little girl feel so special and loved."

"That was my pleasure." He followed her outside and opened her car door as she slid inside then bent down as she started it. "I hope the big girl on today's outing felt special and loved, too."

She reached out a hand and caressed his cheek. "She definitely did, cowboy."

He leaned in for one quick kiss that threatened to fog her windows.

Ellen pulled away with a happy sigh and blew him one more kiss before she shut the car door and drove away with his heart.

Chapter Nine

Ellen strolled along the sidewalk between the office and her apartment on Christmas Eve. A feeling of sweet contentment settled over her like a warm, cozy sweater on a chilly winter day. Christmas cheer surrounded her as she meandered past store windows full of garlands, twinkling lights, and holiday displays.

Her feet carried her to the window of a bookstore full of children's holiday stories. On impulse, she went inside and purchased two books for Missy. In the past few weeks, she'd grown quite attached to the little girl.

Thanks to Burke's efforts, John Hayes had found employment at the truck stop where the manager had allowed him to park his old car. Additionally, Burke had talked his landlord into letting John rent one of the houses he owned not far from the truck stop. It needed a lot of repair work, but was livable. In exchange for the work John promised to do on the place in his spare time, the property owner was willing to waive the rent and purchase the supplies. Burke assured John he'd be willing to help if he ran into projects he couldn't do on his own.

The only thing keeping the season from being perfect was the fact that CPS still hadn't finalized the paperwork releasing Missy back into her father's care.

When Ellen and Burke had gone to visit the little girl yesterday and take her out to see the holiday lights in some of the ritzy neighborhoods in town, she'd been beside herself at not spending Christmas with her father.

Until CPS gave the okay, John was supposed to stay away from his daughter. Burke had done everything he could, and Ellen had pleaded John's case until she was blue in the face, but the person who pushed through the red tape didn't really seem to care. At this point, it looked like it would be sometime in January before the daughter and father would be reunited.

It broke Ellen's heart to see Missy so distraught, but she didn't know what to do about it.

Last week, Burke had insisted they take Missy to visit Santa at the mall. Missy assured them she knew he wasn't the real Santa, just one of the helpers who made sure requests were sent to the North Pole.

With covert maneuvers that impressed Ellen, Burke somehow managed to tuck Missy's letter to Santa in his pocket after she gave it to the mall Santa. Later, after he and Ellen had gone to dinner they returned to her place to watch a movie. Eager to discover what the child most wished to find beneath the tree Christmas morning, they opened the letter and read it. Ellen would have gone to great lengths to purchase whatever toy Missy requested.

Instead, tears sprang to her eyes and Burke kept clearing his throat, as though emotion threatened to choke the air right out of him when they read Missy's letter. The only thing she wanted Santa to bring her was her daddy.

More determined than ever to make her wish a reality, Burke and Ellen had spent hours pleading John's case, but their heartfelt testimony went nowhere.

Resigned to making the best of the situation, Ellen had at least gained permission to take Missy home with her for Christmas Day. Her parents would love having the little girl at their home and Ellen's extended family would make the child feel welcome. They'd even planned a surprise birthday party for Missy, complete with a cake for that afternoon.

Burke had to work, but he promised to join Ellen as soon as he finished his shift.

With plans to see him when he got off this evening, Ellen had arranged a special Christmas Eve dinner for just the two of them.

Somewhere between bumping into Burke back in July and watching him shower Missy with genuine affection and sincere care, she'd fallen in love with the man. Thoughts of him lifted her heart, filled her soul, and made her dream of a long, happy future together. She smiled as she strolled along, envisioning future Christmas celebrations with Burke.

A group of Victorian-attired carolers sang traditional holiday songs in front of a collective of eclectic shops. Ellen stopped and purchased a cup of steaming hot cider from a nearby vendor then joined the crowd in listening to the carolers. Cinnamon and apple aromas wafted up to her as she sipped the warm, spice-laden brew.

In no rush, since she had the afternoon to herself, she continued strolling along, absorbed in the sights, sounds, scents and feelings of Christmas permeating the world around her.

A display in the window of a florist shop drew her interest and she walked over to stand in front of it, amused by the colorful elves and glittering ornaments. The elves drew her thoughts back around to Burke and his teasing references to her as an elf.

Lost in her musings of him, she failed to notice startled shoppers jumping back out of the way of a horse as it raced down the sidewalk, hooves pounding with each stride across the pavement.

Suddenly aware of a disturbance, she turned and watched Burke and Sugar Bear hasten toward her. Ellen's eyes widened as Burke seemed intent on reaching her.

She'd never admit it to anyone, even Tara, that she'd always dreamed of a man riding up to her on a horse and whisking her off into the sunset.

The sunset was a few hours off, but a thrill shot through her as Burke kept his gaze pinned to hers.

"Ellen!" he called when he was just half a block away, waving to her.

She tucked her purchases into the big shoulder bag she carried and returned his wave. Rather than stop, Burke bent down and clasped her upraised hand. He wrapped his other around her waist and hauled her up in front of him on the horse.

"My word, Burke! What are you doing?" she asked, so stunned, she didn't even notice the cheering crowd around them or the fact she'd wrapped her arms around him, pressing so close, she could practically taste the delicious fragrance of his skin.

"Saving Mistletoe," he said, and urged the horse to go faster. Instead of fighting through the crowded sidewalks, he guided the horse into the street, speeding past cars until he guided Sugar Bear onto a side street. An officer met them there and took Sugar Bear while Burke guided Ellen toward his pickup parked nearby.

"Burke? What do you mean saving Mistletoe?" Ellen asked as he helped her into his pickup and rushed around to slide behind the wheel.

"She ran away from the foster home. Apparently, she was there at breakfast then said she wanted to go color in her room. When they called her to come down for lunch, she didn't appear. A search of the house found her gone along with her backpack. She left her suitcase." Burke drove through the busy Christmas Eve traffic like a man possessed.

Ellen cringed when he barely missed being clipped by a driver who wasn't paying attention and pulled right in front of him on the narrow downtown street. Burke swerved, driving down the center of the street between the two lanes of traffic and kept going.

Unable to find her voice, she glanced over at Burke. His jaw was set in a determined line and his hands clenched the steering wheel.

She reached over and placed her hand on his leg, giving it a reassuring pat. "It's okay, Burke. We'll find her."

He squeezed her hand then brought her fingers up to his lips, kissing the backs of them before twining their fingers together and resting them on his thigh. "We will." Sheepish, he looked at her. "I'm sorry. I should have called you, should have asked if you wanted to come with me. You mentioned you were going to walk around downtown this afternoon and window-shop, so it wasn't hard to find you. I just assumed…"

"No, Burke. I do want to come. I'm just surprised at the method you chose to bring me along." The smile she offered him hinted at how much she enjoyed it. "You did make quite a spectacle downtown."

"It's Portland. They are used to spectacles in every shape and size."

Ellen laughed. "That's true. Now, how are we going to find Missy?"

"Every available cop who can help is out looking for her. I think it's a safe bet she's going to try to get to the truck stop. She knows her dad is there. In case Missy does make it that far, John is staying there."

"Where do we start?" she asked, watching as Burke took an exit near the neighborhood where Missy's foster family lived.

"Pretend you're six, scared, and mad. You know where the truck stop is, but you might not know how to get there. Where would you go?" Burke asked as he turned onto a side street.

"I'd find a ride, someone who knows the way," Ellen said. She turned to Burke again. "Do you think she has any money? She might try to get a cab to take her somewhere?"

"I don't know. What I do know is that she snuck out of the house, most likely right after breakfast. If it was me, I'd run until my legs got tired, then I'd try to figure out where to go." Burke looked at her. "How far could you run as a kid?"

"That was a while ago, Burke, and I was much more interested in playing with dolls and reading books than running around outside with the neighborhood hooligans." Ellen tried to think back to when she was Missy's age. "Once, Liam and I were playing and he challenged me to a race. One of his friends yelled 'Go!' and we ran and ran and ran. When we both stopped, we were exhausted and lost. My aunt finally had to come looking for us. We were both scared and never did anything like that again."

"Can you recall how far you went?" Burke asked as he turned down another side street.

Ellen realized they wouldn't find Missy on a main thoroughfare. She'd likely try to keep from being spotted, if someone hadn't already picked her up. What if some pervert dragged her into his car. What is she'd been hurt? What if…

After a few calming breaths, Ellen tried to remember how far she'd raced with Liam. "We ran from my aunt's house to the closest drive-in. My aunt bought us ice cream cones after she spent five minutes lecturing us about our poor decision-making skills and scared us both witless with the possibilities of what might happen if we tried anything similar in the future." She looked at Burke. "It was about a mile, I think."

Burke raised an eyebrow her way. "Impressive. You must have some great running legs hiding under those winter clothes." He reached down, like he planned to lift the hem of her long, red plaid skirt.

115

She smacked his hand and pointed to the street in front of them. "If she ran a mile from the foster house, then where would she go?"

"Let's find out," Burke said, driving to the foster house. It was on a dead-end street, so they drove from it to the stop sign, trying to decide which direction Missy might have gone.

"This way," Ellen said, pointing to her right. "She knows we turn this way to go to your house and it's close to the truck stop."

Burke turned right and they drove slowly down the street. "I think she would have just run, not worrying about where. She would have wanted to put distance between her and them before anyone noticed she was gone."

"Okay. Then where?" Ellen glanced around as they neared an intersection.

Burke continued going straight. By now, the sun had been replaced with dusk and the temperature steadily dropped.

"What if she's just gone, Burke? What if she's…"

He kissed her fingers again and gave her a reassuring look. "Don't say it. Don't even think it. Missy has to be fine. That kid… she's… she managed to finagle her way into my heart and if something happened to her…"

Ellen released a tight breath. "Then we'll find her."

Twenty minutes later, Burke checked in to see if anyone had spotted her, or managed to talk to anyone who'd seen her. No one had any clues. Nobody reported seeing a little girl in a green coat with a purple backpack running down a street alone.

They pulled up to a stoplight and Ellen glanced across the street. She sat up, one hand pressing against the dashboard as she strained to see through the dark.

"Burke! Look!" She pointed across the street to a bit of red, barely visible at the base of a tree. The red could have been anything. A Christmas decoration, a leaf bag, a bit of trash, but it was the first twinge of hope she'd experienced since Burke told her Missy was missing. She hoped it was one of Missy's red mittens.

The second the light turned green, Burke roared across the intersection, pulled up on the sidewalk and shone the headlights toward the tree.

Ellen jumped out of the pickup before he brought it to a full stop, racing over to where the little girl curled into a ball with a hand thrown over her eyes to block the light.

"Leave me alone!" Missy shouted swinging her hands, as though she could defend herself against any assailant.

"Missy!" Ellen grabbed one red mitten-covered hand, then the other. "Missy, it's Ellen. Burke and I came to find you!"

"Ellen?" Missy stopped fighting against her and opened her eyes. Tears rolled out of them and across the little cheeks before she launched herself into Ellen's arms, sobbing.

"It's okay, sweetheart. We've got you. You're safe." Burke knelt beside them as he called in the news Missy had been found. He started to take Missy

117

from Ellen, but she refused to turn her loose. While Ellen knelt in the cold grass with the child, Burke placed a call he'd hoped to avoid. Perhaps it was time for a Christmas miracle to set things right.

"Let's get inside the pickup where it's warm," Burke said. He helped Ellen stand as she continued to hold Missy close against her.

"I want my daddy," Missy sobbed. "Please, I just want my daddy."

"I know sweetie," Ellen said, tears filling her eyes.

Burke took Missy and set her inside the pickup then helped Ellen climb onto the seat. Rather than return to the foster home or to the police station, Burke continued driving toward home.

Ellen gave him a questioning glance, but he just nodded his head once and kept driving.

When they pulled off the freeway and turned into the truck stop, Missy looked out the window and squealed. "I love you guys! I get to see my daddy now!"

"You sure do, honey," Burke said.

Missy practically climbed over Ellen in her haste to reach her father. Ellen opened the pickup door and Missy raced toward the door of the truck stop. Before she reached it, John Hayes ran out, swinging his daughter into his arms and raining kisses down on her cheeks.

"Now, that's what I call a Merry Christmas," Burke said, stepping beside Ellen and draping his arm across her shoulders.

She sidled closer to him and smiled. "I agree."

Chapter Ten

Burke handed Ellen a cup of Christmas tea and sank down on the floor beside her. The two of them leaned back against the couch and watched the lights twinkle on his tree. A fire crackled in the fireplace and Christmas music played softly in the background.

Ellen couldn't have envisioned a more perfect, romantic setting, even if the evening hadn't gone anything like she'd planned.

After watching the tearful reunion of Missy and John Hayes, she and Burke had stayed there until the sheriff arrived. He received a call from an unhappy judge who wanted to know the name of the nincompoop at CPS who refused to let a little girl spend Christmas, as well as her birthday, with her father. The judge declared it fine for Missy to stay with John, but did request they make an appearance in his court after the New Year.

Ellen knew good and well it was Burke who made a phone call that resulted in the judge stepping in. When she pressed him about it, all he'd say was that the judge owed him a favor.

Although she expected Burke to have to head back to work to finish his shift, he assured her the officer who took Sugar Bear had agreed to trade shifts, so Burke was now stuck working both Christmas Day and New Year's Eve.

At the moment, Ellen didn't care. Once Missy left with her father, with a promise to see them both tomorrow, Ellen went home with Burke. She'd thought they'd feed Lovey and head back to her apartment, but the rain that started to drizzle right after they arrived at the truck stop turned to snow.

It never snowed in Portland. When it did, the traffic went nuts and people freaked out. The radio announcers encouraged people to get off the roads and stay home, stay wherever they were to avoid being out on the slick roads.

"Our lovely Christmas Eve dinner is waiting in my fridge to be cooked," Ellen said as she took a sip of the fragrant tea.

"We can eat it the day after Christmas," Burke said, handing her a plate full of cookies his mother had mailed him. He'd had to keep Bella from eating them all when she breezed by on her way home from college. Ellen happened to be there that evening and enjoyed meeting Burke's lively young sister. The two women had laughed and joked, mostly at Burke's expense, but they'd definitely hit it off.

Ellen took a peppermint cookie and bit into the soft treat. "Mmm. These are so good. I need to get the recipe from your mom."

"She'd love to share it with you," Burke said, eating a cookie in two bites, then setting the plate back on the coffee table.

He grew quiet and Ellen looked over at him as she took another sip of tea. Smoldering blue eyes clashed with the liquid amber fire burning in hers. He took the cup from her hand and set it on the table before burying his fingers into the silky tresses of her hair.

"I should probably get going," Ellen said, starting to rise. If she stayed any longer, she wasn't sure she could resist the temptation of Burke. His masculine scent mingled with the pine fragrance of the tree and the spicy sweetness of her tea. The room was warm and cozy, the perfect place to wait for Santa or hide from the storm blowing outside.

Burke pulled her back down, settling her across his lap.

"No running away tonight, Elf. Haven't you been listening to the forecast? There's a blizzard blowing outside." Burke smiled at her and she felt her blood begin to heat. "I think you should stay right here, with me. We'll hunker down, under the weather."

"Burke…" she started to protest, but his lips, a scant inch from hers, moved closer, completely distracting her.

"Do you have any idea how beautiful you look in the light from the tree?" he asked before enfolding her in a close embrace that assured her he had no plans to let her go.

Surrendering, she smiled against his neck. "No, but I hope you'll tell me," she whispered.

"Ellen, I know we haven't had much time for dating, at least when it wasn't chaperoned by a bossy six-year-old or one of my four-legged friends, but if you haven't realized it yet, I'm crazy about you. Since you bumped into my life…" He pulled back and grinned at her. "Nothing has been the same."

"And that's a good thing?" she asked, a teasing spark mingling with the yearning in her eyes.

"A very good thing." Burke bracketed her face with his hands. "I love you, Ellen, with all my heart."

"I love you, too, Burke. With all my heart and then some."

He grinned again and pulled her closer. "Merry Christmas, my lovely little elf."

"Merry Christmas, cowboy." Her arms wrapped around his neck while her heart wrapped around their future — together.

Peppermint Cookies

These cookies are easy to make and so fun, especially if you add
  crushed peppermint sprinkles to the tops!

Peppermint Cookies
1 vanilla cake mix
1 small box instant candy cane pudding
2 eggs
1/2 cup butter, softened
1 cup white chocolate chips
1 cup peppermint crunch baking chips

Preheat oven to 350 degrees.

Mix cake mix, pudding, eggs, and butter until well blended. Stir in chips. Drop rounded spoonfuls onto a parchment-lined baking sheet. Bake about six to eight minutes, until cookies are just set (if you poke them, they still give a little but aren't smooshy).

Remove from oven and let cool in pan for a few minutes. At this point, your house will have the most delicious peppermint aroma.

For a bit of fancy, drizzle the tops with vanilla frosting (warm approximately half a cup of frosting in the microwave for about 12 seconds) and sprinkle crushed peppermint on top

NOTE: If you can't find candy cane pudding, use vanilla pudding and a dash of peppermint flavoring. If you can't find peppermint baking chips, use crushed peppermint sticks as a substitute.

Yield: About three dozen.

A Note from the Author

Thank you, dear reader, for coming along on the journey Ellen and Burke took in *Saving Mistletoe*. Don't you just love it when two people come together not just out of a sweet romance, but also for a grand purpose (like helping a little girl find her way back to her father). It was such fun to create these characters, including Sugar Bear and Lovey the dog. If you enjoyed the story, I'd be so appreciative if you'd take just a minute to leave a review.

Interested in learning more about Tara and Brett? Read their story in *Taste of Tara.*

And don't forget to sign up for my newsletter. You'll be able to keep up on the latest releases, enter contests, receive recipes, and be the first to hear exciting news! http://tinyurl.com/shannasnewsletter

Join Shanna Hatfield's mailing list and receive a free short story!

The newsletter comes out once a month
with details about new releases,
sales, recipes, and exclusive contests!
Sign up today!

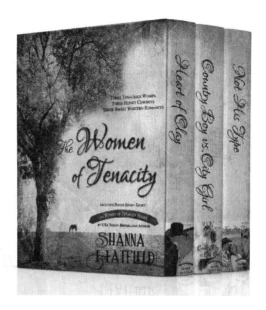

The Women of Tenacity Series

Tenacious, spunky women give the wild, rugged men who love them a run for their money in this contemporary western romance series.

__Heart of Clay__ (Book 1) — Easy-going cowboy Clay Matthews is a respected college professor. He's the man family and friends turn to for help, or when they need a good laugh, since he's a huge tease and practical joker. Life would be almost perfect, except for the strained relationship with his once beloved wife... (*Available **FREE** for electronic downloads.*)

__Country Boy vs. City Girl__ (Book 2) — A confirmed city girl finds herself falling for a wanna-be country boy. Sparks fly as a battle of stubborn will ensues.

The Christmas Cowboy (Book 1) — Among the top saddle bronc riders in the rodeo circuit, easy-going Tate Morgan can handle the toughest horse out there, but trying to handle beautiful Kenzie Beckett is a completely different story.

Wrestlin' Christmas (Book 2) — Sidelined with a major injury, steer wrestler Cort McGraw struggles to come to terms with the end of his career. Shanghaied by his sister and best friend, he finds himself on a run-down ranch with a worrisome, albeit gorgeous widow, and her silent, solemn son.

Capturing Christmas (Book 3) — Life is hectic on a good day for rodeo stock contractor Kash Kressley. Between dodging flying hooves and babying cranky bulls, he barely has time to sleep. The last thing Kash needs is the entanglement of a sweet romance, especially with a woman as full of fire and sass as Celia McGraw.

Barreling Through Christmas (Book 4) — Cooper James might be a lot of things, but beefcake model wasn't something he intended to add to his resume.

Chasing Christmas (Book 5) — Dragged into a crazy publicity stunt, bull rider Chase Jarrett has no idea how he ended up with an accidental bride.

Garden of Her Heart *(Hearts of the War, Book 1)* — The moment the Japanese bombed Pearl Harbor, life shifted for Miko Nishimura. Desperate to reach the Portland Assembly Center for Japanese Americans, she's kicked off the bus miles from town. Every tick of the clock pushes her closer to becoming a fugitive in the land of her birth. Exhausted, she stumbles to her grandparents' abandoned farm only to find a dying soldier sprawled across the step. Unable to leave him, she forsakes all else to keep him alive.

After crashing his plane in the Battle of the Atlantic, the doctors condemn Captain Rock Laroux to die. Determined to meet his maker beneath a blue sky at his family home, he sneaks out of the hospital. Weary and half out of his mind, he makes it as far as a produce stand he remembers from his youth. Rather than surrender to death, Rock fights a battle of the heart as he falls in love with the beautiful Japanese woman who saves his life.

ABOUT THE AUTHOR

SHANNA HATFIELD spent ten years as a newspaper journalist before moving into the field of marketing and public relations. Self-publishing the romantic stories she dreams up in her head is a perfect outlet for her lifelong love of writing, reading, and creativity. She and her husband, lovingly referred to as Captain Cavedweller, reside in the Pacific Northwest.

Shanna loves to hear from readers.
Connect with her online:
Blog: shannahatfield.com
Facebook: Shanna Hatfield's Page
Pinterest: Shanna Hatfield
Email: shanna@shannahatfield.com

If you'd like to know more about the characters in any of her books,
visit the Book Characters page on her website
or check out her **Book Boards** on Pinterest.

Made in the USA
Lexington, KY
10 June 2018